THE RED TIE

Cb

Other Books by Ian Gouge

Novels and Novellas

17 Alma Road - Coverstory books, 2024
Tilt - Coverstory books, 2023
Once Significant Others - Coverstory books, 2023
On Parliament Hill - Coverstory books, 2021
A Pattern of Sorts - Coverstory books, 2020
The Opposite of Remembering - Coverstory books, 2020
At Maunston Quay - Coverstory books, 2019
An Infinity of Mirrors - Coverstory books, 2018 (2nd ed.)
The Big Frog Theory - Coverstory books, 2018 (2nd ed.)
Losing Moby Dick and Other Stories - Coverstory books, 2017

Short Stories

An Irregular Piece of Sky - Coverstory books, 2023
Degrees of Separation - Coverstory books, 2018
Secrets & Wisdom - Paperback, 2017

Poetry

Grimsby Docks - Coverstory books, 2024
Crash - Coverstory books, 2023
not the Sonnets - Coverstory books, 2023
Selected Poems: 1976-2022 - Coverstory books, 2022
The Homelessness of a Child - Coverstory books, 2021
The Myths of Native Trees - Coverstory books, 2020
First-time Visions of Earth from Space - Coverstory books, 2019
After the Rehearsals - Coverstory books, 2018
Punctuations from History - Coverstory books, 2018
Human Archaeology - Coverstory books, 2017
Collected Poems (1979-2016) - KDP, 2017

Non-Fiction

Shrapnel from a Writing Life - Coverstory books, 2022

IAN GOUGE

THE RED TIE

Coverstory books

First published in paperback & ebook
format by Coverstory books, 2024

ISBN 978-1-7384693-5-2 (Paperback)
ISBN 978-1-7384693-6-9 (eBook)

iangouge.substack.com

coverstorybooks.com

Marcus tested his bonds once again, trying to keep his shoulders relaxed as he did so, not wishing to betray his efforts. He felt discomfort at his wrists, pressure from the frame of the chair. Although he knew nothing would have changed in the previous five minutes, there was something in the futility of trying to free himself that kept him centred. The man sitting before him — a smallish weaselly individual — was talking. There was a small table in the space between them.

"…so of course your outcome is decided."

"My 'outcome'?"

"What will become of you."

"Is that so?" Marcus paused, making it plain there was more to be said. He sensed a bluff designed to encourage confession. "So why am I here, trussed up like this, if everything is fixed?"

The Weasel looked over to the corner of the room near the door where a younger man sat, observing. He was just out of Marcus's eye-line.

"You see, Will," said the interrogator, "how clever our friend here is? Clever is dangerous, is it not? A word of advice: never aspire to be duplicitous or clever."

"Is 'clever' supposed to be a compliment?" was what Marcus wanted to say, but refrained; his earlier question still hanging between them.

"What will become of you *publicly*. Is that better?"

Marcus inclined his head. "Which is — as if I didn't know?"

"Different words for pretty much the same thing: conviction; disappearance; execution."

The Weasel's savouring of the final four syllables was self-indulgent, unnecessary. Marcus hoped he would come across him later, under more propitious circumstances. Again he tried to relax his shoulders, his wrists.

"And the other?" he asked

"What other?"

"If that is to be my public fate, then what about the non-public one. You implied there was another side to the equation."

Standing, the Weasel made a slow circuit of the table. From over Marcus's shoulder: "Clever, Will, see? Our friend here."

The young man in the corner said nothing. Marcus waited. After a few moments — time punctuated by soft footfall on the faux oak flooring — the small man reappeared in front of Marcus, resumed his seat.

"The same. Or different. A little like your books, Professor; the public version and what lay beneath them."

"You mean the original text."

"You know very well what I mean." A trace of anger surfaced in the Weasel's tone.

"How different?" Marcus tried to diffuse it, knowing his captor was keen to speak, revelling in his position of power, however transient.

"Because of your choice. Simple as that." Unable to disguise his agitation, the Weasel stood once more and walked the three paces to the far wall where he turned. There was a slight change of tone. "You know — because you are so clever, Professor — that much of our case is circumstantial. There is some evidence, clearly; after all, you have been editing these books of yours for long enough, getting your messages out." Marcus wanted to interrupt and protest that the books were never his, but kept his counsel. "Subtle, never totally explicit. You must be aware that there are — what shall I say? — differences of opinion?"

"Because of what I'm given, what I have to work with?"

"Partly. And so the voice we hear — 'voice' is a term you clever book-people use, is it not? — the voice may or may not be yours, may or may not be that of the original writer."

Again Marcus wanted to correct him, tell him the word he should use was 'author', but he did not. "I can see how that presents you with something of a dilemma," he said instead. "I have taught as much to my students. From time-to-time anyway. How can you know which is which?"

A laugh. "*You* can know, my dear Professor; you can know."

"Indeed; but that doesn't really help you — or your young friend in the corner."

The Weasel looked toward the silent young man for a moment. "Will? He's just learning the ropes. 'Work experience', you might say."

"The Master and the Apprentice, Mr. Simpson?"

Bowing slightly, the inquisitor offered acknowledgement — and Marcus instantly knew that he had missed both the literary allusion and the sarcasm.

"But there is simply too much evidence — if I may continue to use that word — for comfort. Too much suspicion. Too much potential cleverness. Hence the Ministry has decided that you need to be — withdrawn."

"Publicly," Marcus prompted.

"Indeed."

"And privately?"

The Weasel paused for a moment, then resumed his seat before speaking. "In your case — for whatever reason — there remains the potential for some difference to exist between fiction and fact. Is that a suitable way of expressing it? I think that's highly appropriate, don't you?"

"The public is the fiction?"

"The public *may* be the fiction. If we do indeed execute you, then there is only fact, is there not? The fiction evaporates."

Marcus wanted to ask him if he had been reading his lecture notes, but again refrained. He knew he was listening to a man essentially struggling, a man out of his depth. Behind him he heard the young man shift in his chair. "And all that depends on?"

"In its wisdom, the Ministry has decided that although the public outcome is settled — there will be an announcement made tomorrow as part of the Monday bulletin — what actually transpires may be different."

"Depending on?"

"Depending on you, my dear Professor!" As if the entire conversation had been building to this point, the Weasel laughed again. It was a laugh underpinned by nervousness, by fear of repercussions, and an uncertainty over consequential outcomes many years hence. "There is 'an opportunity' for you to change sides."

"Poacher turned gamekeeper?"

"If you like."

"Always assuming that I was a poacher in the first place."

"Which you are."

"Which you accuse me of being." Marcus corrected him.

"Have it your way." There was a pause as Simpson checked his watch. "You have — and of this we are indeed certain — 'connections'; whether you are a subversive or not (and at this stage that is more or less irrelevant), you have links to those who *are* anti-state, rebellious, traitors. We know that you know people..." Another pause. "On that basis, and irrespective of what I myself might think, I am authorised to make you this offer — which, incidentally, is one of the other reasons Will is here, to act as witness — the offer of immunity in return for continuing to work for the Ministry, though in an entirely different capacity. Something more 'proactive', you might say. We will provide you with a new identity, a new home for you and your family, the opportunity for you to redeem yourself. All in exchange for a minor sacrifice or two elsewhere — painless, as far as you are concerned. That is your choice."

Marcus recognised how difficult it was for the Weasel to make this offer; given a free hand, he might just as easily have pulled out a pistol and shot him there and then. He felt the rope on his wrists; his fingers caressed the back of the chair as if to remind himself what feeling things was like.

Simpson was staring hard at him as if unprepared to release his gaze until he had his answer. Marcus told himself that he would never forget the Weasel's face.

Then he gave his answer.

Behind him the door to room 1.51 opened.

❉

When he looks out of his kitchen window each morning the view is always the same: wrapped around his small courtyard garden, the dark evergreen hedge whose colour varies little with the seasons. It is a hedge which always seems to need trimming somewhere. This time of year there is nothing cheery or uplifting about it, nothing celebratory; the winter mornings are so dark for so long that most often the hedge appears to be nothing other than black, its leaves virtually invisible as if they had been absorbed by the night.

This particular morning he sighs as he probably does most mornings in January. Not only does it already feel as if it has been winter forever, but the sameness of his routine overwhelms him: switch on the light, fill the kettle, prepare his breakfast. Then stare out of the window as he waits for the hot water, the toast. Some days he tries to vary the routine — perhaps put the toast on before boiling the kettle, or opt for coffee rather than tea — but the sequence makes little difference; they are still things he is forced to endure. Then, at the end of the ritual, after his perfunctory eating and drinking, he will go back upstairs to the bathroom and finish his ablutions, choose a tie from his very limited selection. At this point on most days, Monday to Friday, he tells himself he will go out at the weekend and buy a new tie, one that isn't blue. It will be a statement tie. His colleagues will see him the following week sporting a yellow or green one, or one with a vibrant paisley pattern, and they will wonder what was going on, draw conclusions, ask him who the lucky girl is (because for many of the men he works with, women are the reason for everything).

But today, this Friday, things are different. Breakfast may have been the same and the hedge appeared identical, but for once he does not have to go to work; he does not have to choose which blue tie to wear. Verna had called them into her office just before they left the previous evening and told them they would not be needed; there was some kind of inspection scheduled which would so disrupt the normal working of their department. Consequently management had decided to give certain individuals — those not needed by the auditors — the day off. With pay. It had taken him the entirety of the tram-ride home to process the information and, even then, left him vaguely unsettled all evening. A day to himself. And an unexpected and unplanned one. Perhaps it would give him the opportunity to finally go and buy that tie.

Having finished cleaning his teeth, he stares at himself in the mirror, undertaking the examination almost as if he were a hedge. Like the evergreen, his is a visage which has barely changed. Yes, the face is gradually ageing, but it is doing so imperceptibly; and on occasion, like the hedge, he too needs a trim, both of his hair (which he worries is beginning to thin) and his beard, which he returns to its sharply defined best every Sunday morning. He can do nothing about his hair of course — not in terms of how thick it is — but the beard is an entirely different matter. It had been cultivated as part of a somewhat lacklustre office initiative when most of the men decided to abstain from shaving for a month in order to raise money for the widow of a member of the finance department who had unexpectedly died. At the end of the month virtually all newly-grown beards were removed, the effect being that, on the Monday following, it was as if half the staff in the office had been replaced by newer and younger versions of those who had previously been working there. For some reason he had decided to keep his. He believed it endowed him with gravitas; others thought it made him look old before his time. In the two years since then he has nurtured it with care. Now it is as much a part of him as the hedge is part of his meagre garden or a blue tie part of his work uniform.

When he looks in the mirror he also does so knowing there will be no-one creeping into view behind him; just as there is no-one with whom to share breakfast, nor split the chores attendant on part-owning a small house with a small yard and an over-large hedge. Like most single men of a certain age, he has a limited range of excuses to apply to his domestic solitude, the most common of these being that he has yet to meet the right woman. Given current cultural norms, what was once called 'playing the field' is more or less frowned upon, and this, in consequence, applies pressure on individuals to ensure they make the 'least worst' choice of partner at the first attempt. This imperative also feeds into his explanation for his solitude. He has known people who have rushed into partnership and regretted it within weeks; indeed, he works with one or two of these unhappy souls. Increasingly rare is the kind of kinship witnessed between that departed finance colleague and the widow he left behind. Perhaps his keeping of the beard is a tribute to that. Most people seem satisfied to rub along reasonably well, yet he has always told himself that achieving nothing more than the emotionally average is hardly ambitious. Old fashioned it may be (indeed it may even be a manifestation of fear) but there is a part of him that chooses to remain faithful to the notion of love and kismet, and this — along with his instinctive caution and introspection — is perhaps the primary reason that, aged nearly forty, he remains conspicuously unattached.

Not that he is a naturally ambitious character; both academic and work records demonstrate as much. Marginally sub-par educationally, his choices when it came to post-college employment were somewhat limited, and he settled on the Ministry's publishing function as the most palatable of the options presented to him. Over time he discovered that his eye for detail was valuable to them. Initially this involved checking texts for grammar and syntax, and that authors had not strayed too far from permissible language. If the book under scrutiny was non-fiction and a matter of historical record, then the truth needed to be adhered to. Like all Ministry departments, they used artificial intelligence for much of the grunt-work — even to the extent of having it write some of the less complex books — then discovered that computers, however clever, lacked nuance and human instinct, and that in order to produce the most engaging books people still needed to be involved. Adept at manipulating the AI interface, he had become one of the main controllers, a prestigious if not senior role, and an appointment which suited him perfectly well. In non-fiction he had been happy enough doing a good job and expanding his knowledge along the way.

Whether his employers had regarded it as some kind of reward he is unable to say, but for just under two years he has been assigned to fiction. The grammar-checking part was initially problematic given he was instinctively inclined to be far too rigid in his linguistic assessment. When some of the authors complained, he expected to be returned to work on non-fiction; yet they persevered with him, gave him more time, more training, and an opportunity to improve his reading. Gradually he found more appropriate ways to use the AI tools at his disposal, then he started to use them less, became attuned to an author's style and voice more readily, and understood what — in terms of grammar — he could let go. Complaints fell away. After six months everyone seemed happy.

Everyone except him.

The reason for his discomfort was simple enough. Where he had been at home in the certain world of facts, of names and dates, with events of record, the fabricated stories in the texts he had been asked to process confused him. In the early days he read fiction as if it were fact, would consult the National Record to check on the veracity of incidents depicted. His was a move from a world where there was indisputably a 'right' and 'wrong', to one where everything was false. Those early months had been dark, and even as he progressed in terms of technique and understanding, during the first year he was never entirely comfortable. Historical novels — those blending fiction within proven historical context — confused him most of all.

Yet it is not this confusion (admittedly occurring less frequently now) which is the source of his current disquiet; rather it is one of belief. In the old days he had been able to trust what he read and, trusting it, accept it as fact. It was a kind of learning by rote. But now, even though he understands that he should not believe everything he reads, he worries that in his editing he runs the risk of inadvertently turning fiction into fact. He tries to comfort himself with the knowledge that he will filter out anything malevolent or misleading prior to public consumption, adhere to the yardstick by which he and the rest of the population have been navigating successfully for at least forty years now. And it *has* been a success; anyone can see that. There have been no wars in all that time, no famine, no major disasters other than natural ones — and it is common knowledge that the incidence of those has been on the wane for some time. These are facts; he has worked on the books which prove as much. Yet occasionally he comes across things in draft novels — hidden deep within the text — which hint at a different kind of truth. It is never much more than a whisper: there is nothing to be pulled out of the text, no specific words to which he can point or edit away; the narratives are always coherent and believable and — most importantly — acceptable. He cannot recall any of the novels he worked on ever being recalled because he missed something problematic. Surely there is some reassurance to be garnered from that?

❉

There are two types of tram which run throughout the town. The modern ones are sleek and silent, brightly lit and clean, with generous doors and low thresholds which make them easy to enter and exit. The fastest of the fleet, they are used on the newest and busiest routes, where the roads are at their widest, and where the volume of commuters from the suburbs is at its greatest. In some places fresh tracks (independent of the roads) have been laid to accommodate them, but most of their city centre routes run through the streets, sharing them with cars and lorries, cyclists and pedestrians.

The older variety of tram are mechanically the exact opposite: old and narrow, badly lit and cold, and difficult to enter via steep steps at either end. These rattle along, and you can often hear them coming before you can see them, their bells — employed by drivers to warn of their approach — sounding more like apologetic coughs than anything else. Many were daubed with graffiti long ago, and although this has been outlawed and a programme of repainting and refurbishment embarked upon, those that remain blemished retain what some residents like to think of as their 'old character'. On that basis, the refurbishment programme has been allowed to wane, the money diverted by the Ministry's transport department into other forms of maintenance. The combination of both old and new trams weaving through the streets is regarded by many as one of the city's great charms, and whenever the Ministry produces anything approaching promotional literature for tourists (not that there have been very many since the borders were more or less closed) images of the trams — both new and old — loom large.

From where he lives he can take two trams into the centre of the city. The number 14 is one of the newer variety. Stopping just five times along the way, it is able to deposit him in the main square in twenty minutes. It is rarely late. The alternative is line 10, serviced by some of the most aged trams in the fleet. Its route is somewhat ponderous, winding its way through the old town; it stops many more times, and takes at least thirty minutes to arrive at the same place. Often its journey-time is significantly extended either because of traffic jams in the narrower streets or by accidents most often caused by cyclists getting their wheels stuck in the tracks and being thrown into the path of an oncoming vehicle of one sort or another. Fatalities are, thankfully, few and far between.

Unless he is running late, he always takes the 10. He has a soft spot for the rattling old carriages; there is a certain nostalgia about them, even if it is from a time he can only dimly remember. As a child, riding the trams had been something of a rarity given the family lived close both to where his father worked and to all the shops his mother needed. Everything — including his school — was within a few minutes walk of their house. And it is not just the old trams themselves he likes, but the journey; there is something special about the experience of being aboard a lumbering beast as it weaves its way through the narrow single-lane streets, past the small Botanical Gardens, the ruins of the Catholic cathedral, and the area which had once been home to various types of artisan. The latter — still referred to as 'the Makers' Quarter' — now boasts few such establishments: two jewellers, an umbrella-maker, a milliner. Some of the old shops have been turned into 'bijou' restaurants (where few can afford to eat), and there had been a half-hearted attempt a few years previously to rebrand the area as 'the Restaurant Quarter'. But the effort had not been persistent enough nor the restaurants of sufficient quantity or quality to keep up their side of the bargain. Even so it remains the area of the city he likes best, and on his way into town this Friday morning he plans to descend from the tram two stops early and head for his favourite café. Why should he not take such an opportunity on a rare day off?

Although he had woken at his normal time, he ends up taking the number 10 some two hours later than usual, the time in between used for household chores: putting some washing in the machine, sweeping the kitchen and hall floors, preparing the vegetables for his dinner then setting his slow-cooker to work. The consequence of his dallying is that when he enters the tram he finds he has a choice of seat, in stark contrast to his working-day experience when he most often needs to stand all the way. It is a prospect so unusual that he pauses at the top of the steps — long enough to get a push in the back from a more impatient traveller. The few faces that turn his way on hearing the woman's complaint are all foreign to him. He is used to recognising a large proportion of his fellow commuters even when the morning tram is full; indeed, he is on nodding acquaintance with a few of them. The people on this particular Friday tram are of a different order however: they are older, somehow shabbier, and self-evidently less professional. They look less like people with a purpose, and more like those who can think of nothing better to do. Categorising them thus, as he takes a window seat about half-way back he wonders for a moment what they might make of him, convinced that because of his age, the slightly better cut of his clothes, he must stand out from them. More than that, he has an objective: he is going to buy a non-blue tie.

Mesmerised by the view through his window for the next few stops, it is some minutes later when he bothers to scan inside the tram again. Its occupants have hardly changed. The woman who pushed past him and had been sitting across the aisle is no longer there, her place taken by a younger woman who — based on her age alone — also seems somewhat out of place. Although she is looking out onto her side of the street, for a moment he has the oddest sensation that she has been looking his way; indeed, he wonders if it had been her gaze which had somehow been the trigger for him to divert his attention from the passing urban landscape. For a few seconds he examines her, then, convinced he has been imagining things, looks out again just in time to see the entrance to the Botanical Gardens come into view. Two more stops and he will be getting off.

A grey morning, it has been threatening to rain ever since he left the house. His instinctive glance toward the sky when he steps down from the tram is therefore entirely within reason, as is the lifting of his coat collar before he walks the seventy-five metres or so to the entrance of "The Runcible Spoon". Set in an irregular terrace of mismatched buildings, their doors hard onto an uneven pavement, it is a somewhat quirky establishment, perfectly in-tune with both the location and its unusual name. Thanks to inadequate internal ventilation, the windows onto the street are constantly fogged with condensation, and therefore the only way in which to appreciate the interior is to actually step through the door. A small café, it boasts just ten round wooden tables, each with three matching chairs set against them. The matching comes not from their style but the primary colours the furniture is painted. All perfectly arranged on his entrance — red table with red chairs, blue alongside blue — he knows that after a particularly busy day there will be a more kaleidoscopic effect as chairs will have been moved throughout. But it being early — and a working day — the regimented pattern currently remains intact. With only one of the tables taken, he chooses a green one near the window and sits down, briefly rubbing a small section of the glass with his sleeve before he removes his coat. Able to look out for a few minutes, when the condensation eventually returns he knows he will have to wipe the glass again.

He orders a slice of Bostock and a milky coffee. Both are treats. Rarely indulging in pastries, the almond bread is one of his favourites. As a single man living alone he has little use for milk, and therefore almost always takes his coffee black. The coffee at "The Runcible Spoon" is, in his opinion, exceptional and justifies the more luxurious beverage. At various locations on the walls around the café are posters of fantastic beasts which he knows from previous enquiry are derived from the fiction of other nations. He has often wondered what he would do if such a work landed on his desk, what he would need to look out for when it came to the validation process — after all, if it was all fantasy, from where would he obtain his frame of reference?

It is while he is engaged in an absentminded review of the café's decoration that the brass bell above the door rings and drags his attention away from contemplation of what he assumes is a Griffin. Pausing on the threshold is the young woman who had been sitting across from him on the tram. She glances around the room before heading towards the orange table which is set against the wall just behind his own. Unable to stop himself from doing so, he tries to plot her recent movements, assuming that she must have left the tram at the next stop and walked back. It wouldn't have taken her long, given the relative proximity of some of the stops, but if she had wanted to come to "The Runcible Spoon" why hadn't she got off at the same time as him?

Returning to his half-eaten Bostock, he is drawn to two figures on the pavement attempting to look into the café, and then by the rumble of a tram heading away from the centre of town. Once he has finished his coffee it will take him less than ten minutes to walk to the Market Square. The shop he has in mind in which to buy his tie is located on a quiet side street flanked on one side by a tobacconist and on the other by the offices of a firm of accountants.

"Excuse me."

The voice coming from beside him, he assumes it is the waitress wanting to know if he would like anything else. Then he realises it is the woman at the next table who has spoken. He twists slightly in his seat in order to face her a little more directly. She is leaning forward, smiling.

"Sorry. This is slightly odd, obviously — but, do I know you?"

He tries a smile which he immediately knows is somehow unsatisfactory. "I don't think so. The tram, perhaps?"

Leaving it as a question, he expects to see instant recognition flash across her face, perhaps accompanied by a degree of embarrassment. Instead she frowns.

"No, not really. I mean, I thought I recognised you on the tram, but I couldn't place where I knew you from."

"Really?"

"When I saw you get off it only took a few moments for me to realise that I simply had to satisfy my curiosity, so I got off at the next stop and walked back in the hope of finding you."

"And you did," he says, glancing around the room before returning his gaze to her. "Though it would have been difficult to see me through the window."

"It was," she smiles again, "but I recognised you by the flash of your blue scarf." He follows her eyes to where the scarf and his coat now rest on the chair alongside him. "Not that I do this sort of thing very often you understand." She blushes. "Or ever, actually. But you know; curiosity and all that."

And he does. Part of his job relates to satisfying curiosity. When he comes across something in a manuscript about which he is unsure he is often compelled to verify that what is being said is accurate. Either that or to confirm that it is in accord with the textual guidelines within which he has to work. On that basis all he can do is nod.

"Perhaps we work in the same building," she suggests. "I'm relatively new to the city, so maybe that's it."

"It could be," he concedes, finding himself drawn in, "though my department at the Ministry is a relatively small one."

"The Ministry!" She is unable to conceal her relief. "I work there too! Perhaps I have seen you there, or outside on the street, going to and fro as it were."

"Yes, that's possible."

"But you're not there today?"

"I've been given the day off. Well, most of the department has."

She is suddenly animated. "What a coincidence; so have we! An audit of some kind; that's what we were told."

"Yes, exactly that. I'd assumed it was just our little section, but perhaps it's more wide-ranging than that. I think they do that sometimes."

"And what is it you do there?" As she edges her chair a little closer, he realises he is committed to seeing the conversation through.

"I work in the publishing department." He keeps the explanation simple. "I'm a controller there."

"Really! Isn't that a terribly important job?"

Attempting to examine her as if she is a character in a draft novel, he defines her as perhaps early- to mid-thirties, a little on the petite side, with her brown hair cut fashionably short. The brown seems a little too dark, and so he wonders if she has tinted it towards black. Either way, she has the complexion to carry it off. Though she is attractive and reasonably well-dressed, he wonders if she is largely unremarkable — at least in the sense of a fiction — though there is something in her tone of voice and the slight thinness of her lips to suggest she could be resolute if she was put to the test.

"Important? Well, it certainly has its responsibilities. We have to ensure that books are historically and factually accurate. It would be unacceptable if we allowed things that were untrue to masquerade as fact."

"Oh, I agree! Is that what you work with then, history and the like?"

"It's where I used to work."

"Used to?"

"I've been in fiction well over a year now."

She places one hand over her mouth as she moves back a little in her chair. Then she leans forward even further. "But that's even more of a responsibility! And such a difficult job."

"Oh?" He finds himself warming to the exchange. "And why do you say that?"

"Because it's all made-up — the stories, I mean. If someone writes a history and says something happened twenty years ago, it either did or didn't. Isn't that right? But with fiction... How can you know?"

He laughs softly at her amazement. "Well you can't of course."

"So that makes it difficult, right?" She shifts her chair a little closer such that she has almost joined him at his table, his green furniture compromised by her orange chair.

"A lot of the time it doesn't matter because the stories are so fantastical or so obviously made-up. A couple of months ago I worked on a novel that was pure science fiction, a story about another world. How can you possibly verify what happens on imaginary planets?" He lifts his cup only to realise it is empty.

"But what about the more domestic stories? Or those with 'messages'?"

"'Domestic'?"

"You know, stories set in the here and now, about real people, their lives and so forth?"

"There are things you can check. You'd be surprised. For example, we have tools to help us ensure the stories are not about real people who have just been recreated in some flimsy disguise; after all, that wouldn't do at all would it? How would you like it if you read a book and found that one of the characters in it was you?"

She laughs, clearly amused by the notion. It is a trigger for him to check his watch.

"Oh, I'm keeping you." She is suddenly embarrassed again. "I'm so sorry."

"Things to do," he says, standing and reaching for his coat. "I'm off to town to buy a new tie."

"That's nice. And it's better to go shopping on a Friday rather than a Saturday." She stands. "My name's Marina, by the way."

His right arm in the appropriate sleeve, he finishes pulling on his coat then tugs the blue scarf from the back of the chair.

"Vincent," and he extends his hand which she takes warmly.

❈

Less than ten minutes later Vincent has arrived in the Market Square. With the Ministry situated on one of the main adjoining roads, it's familiar enough territory, though he's used to being there when people are rushing to and from work, or at lunchtime amidst the general bustle for food and the like. There are a number of small bars and entertainment venues nearby, and the area still has a reputation for being 'lively' on Saturday evenings — though he cannot vouch for that personally. Seeing the square mid-way through a Friday morning, he is struck by how different it feels. It is a sensation manifest not simply in the fewer people present, but how they look and move, their lack of urgency, the absence of noise. When a tram rings its bell, the sound echoes across the square and bounces from the facades of the buildings.

Vincent slackens his place to browse in a number of shop windows. At some point he will need to get some new boots and, on looking into a shoe shop, is surprised to see not only how costly they have become, but how little choice there seems to be. Then, resisting the temptation to venture into the bookshop next door (after all, they know him there!) he settles on looking in through their window, attempting to spot volumes on which he has worked. He sees a few, but again is taken aback by the fact that the books are more expensive than he remembers. Unsettled, he makes his way across the square, into the relevant side street, and past the accountants. The window of the menswear store is almost entirely empty, an employee mid-way through re-dressing it. Two mannequins stand unadorned, and in one corner three large boxes look as if they are waiting to be opened.

Inside there is a warm kind of hush, as if the environment has been designed to envelop and cosset its customers. Vincent pauses and takes a breath during which time an assistant, having marked his entry, is already heading his way.

"Good morning, Sir. How can I help you?"

Vincent doesn't feel as if he needs any help; he just wants to find the ties and see what they have on offer. His default has always been to ask for help only as and when he needs it, but now the other man is immediately in front of him and he has no wish to appear rude.

"I'm looking for a new tie."

"Ah," smiles the assistant, then, turning on his heel, says "if you'll follow me."

"Just browsing, you know," Vincent offers to the other man's back.

"Quite so."

He trails the assistant past two rails of trousers, one of jackets, the wall to his left adorned with small box-like shelves within which an array of shirts nestles. Most are white, the rest plain and tending towards the paler end of the spectrum. Just beyond the jackets is a single carousel of ties. Although it has been some time since he has been in the store, Vincent is sure he remembers them having at least three times as many.

"Ties, sir. For work perhaps?"

Momentarily thrown by the other man's slightly rising inflection, Vincent allows his right hand to brush through those on the side of the display immediately facing him.

"Yes," he says, then turns the carousel slowly clockwise in order to examine the remainder. They are nearly all blue.

"Were you looking for anything in particular, sir?"

Vincent is fingering two ties in turn, both identical to ones he has at home.

"I was hoping for something a little different colour-wise. Or with a more striking pattern."

"I'm afraid these are all we have at the moment." The assistant offers an apologetic wave of the hand.

"But I remember your selection being so much greater." Vincent wants to say 'more than just blue' but refrains from doing so.

"Yes." The man hesitates for just a heartbeat. "Recent instructions from Head Office, I'm afraid. Apparently there isn't the demand any more. Across the range."

Vincent is struck at the oddness of the phrase. He lets his hands fall.

"Then I think I'll leave it for now. I'm afraid I don't need another blue tie."

"I perfectly understand, sir."

As he turns, Vincent has the sensation not only that he is being allowed to leave, but that some kind of transaction — if only of understanding — has passed between them.

"Thanks for your help anyway."

On his way to the front door Vincent can't help but notice the cctv cameras embedded in the ceiling. Taking his eyes from where he is walking, he inadvertently collides with one of the rails and, in order to cover his embarrassment, makes a show of examining the trousers and jackets it contains. They are either blue, black or grey; the shirts nearby white, pale blue, or creme. He dawdles just a little to see if he can get a glimpse of something other; a flash of green or pink perhaps, the hint of check or herringbone. But there is none.

The assistant, now back at the counter, looks up from the journal in which he has begun to write, nods but says nothing.

✳

"I think what was decided on was entirely reasonable; do you not agree?"

Mid-way down a long panelled corridor on the third floor of the Ministry two men are walking side-by-side, heads slightly bowed as they speak, their voices barely above a whisper.

"Entirely logical," says the second and taller of the two. Both are grey-suited, a small emblem stitched into the fabric of their black ties.

"And of course unanimous," replies the shorter man. He is wearing round spectacles, their dark frames in stark contrast to the whiteness of his skin.

"It was never not going to be so. And now that we're starting to get some data through in terms of buying trends, well — it demonstrates the policy is working."

"Does it?"

The tall man — who has been entirely focussed on where he has been placing his feet — glances to his companion.

"Don't get me wrong," the bespectacled man clarifies. "I'm merely suggesting that it may still be too early to say. That's all. Yes, the data is giving us an indication that things may be calming down a little — if I may use that phrase — but it's not conclusive yet. And we can't lose sight of the fact that — in the grand scheme — these are just small measures. Very small measures."

"Indeed; like when we banned hoodies." The tall man resumes his concentration on his feet. "But it's all about momentum. Or breaking momentum. Just as the Prefect said. And it's the only way to go about such things, with some caution; it's not as if we're monsters."

As if it was a private joke, the phrase makes the shorter man laugh. "Hopefully those days are long behind us — not that I choose to remember them that often."

"Nor I."

"Lessons were learned though, wouldn't you say?"

"Isn't that the purpose of history?" Although a question, the taller man's tone suggests statement rather than enquiry.

"That all depends on which books you read."

They both laugh.

✼

There are individuals who — even when they are on a day's holiday — might be tempted to drop into their office should they find themselves in close enough proximity to it. On leaving the outfitters and regaining the square, Vincent is near enough to the Ministry to be able to see the beginnings of the complex, yet he is not the sort of individual to 'drop in' anywhere. Had he been closer to his colleagues (emotionally that is) he might have been inclined to wander down and see who was in; but he is not made that way — and in any event, as far as he can recall, only Fran and Noah have been excluded from the bonus long-weekend. As departmental administrator, Fran is always up to her neck in paperwork, chasing progress on this book or that, liaising with printers and libraries, bookshops and other departments. Or she is running errands for Verna. She could hardly be spared. And Noah? He has been told that the deadline for the volume on which he is working has been tightened and therefore also couldn't be spared; indeed, he might be required to work part of the weekend too. Whether Vincent found that demand more surprising than Noah he can't possibly say. The book on which Noah is working is a textbook that has recently been upgraded to become required reading for a level-2 science examination — and now the date for the national exams have been brought forward by two weeks. Hence the pressure. When Noah found out, his reaction had been to raise his eyebrows (his favoured mode of non-verbal expression) and say "well, who would have guessed?", as if he had known all along that something would stymie his chance for an extra day off. Aided by the use of his eyebrows, such fatalism is also part of Noah's make-up.

Like Vincent, he had begun working in non-fiction; then, after three years, was moved into children's books. Not having sufficient empathy or insight to be an effective controller there, he was given a chance in fiction for a short while before being moved back to non-fiction, specifically focussing on dry educational texts. It had been Noah's post Vincent had filled when he moved into fiction.

"They can't trust me there," he had said to Vincent during a quiet moment in their brief handover.

"Trust?" At the time, Vincent didn't entirely understand how trust could be relevant when it came to made-up stories. In non-fiction yes, especially as it was important to get the facts right; but in fiction?

"That's why they want me somewhere safe like school and college books where there's a right and wrong answer, and where opinions don't matter."

They had all been through copious training in relation to opinion and belief, and controllers were provided with multiple techniques for recognising and then eradicating their personal selves from the work. Their duty was to give readers the most accurate and appropriate books they could, not to insert themselves into them.

"You must have noticed," Noah had said to him another time when they were on a coffee break, his voice lowered even though in the Ministry's vast canteen it was almost drowned out by the clink of cutlery and thrum of background chatter.

"Noticed what?"

"All those things that aren't in the books — especially the histories."

"How can I notice something that isn't there?" Vincent had laughed.

"Ah, you've the perfect profile to work in fiction my friend!"

*

"Hello again!"

Vincent glances up from his coffee to find Marina standing in front of him.

"I thought it was you," she continues as she places her tray on his table.

"How did you find me?" He looks out across the throng knowing it is impossible to locate anyone in the canteen unless you had made a prior arrangement as to roughly where you would be sitting.

"Just luck," she says cheerfully. "I happened to be a few people behind you in the queue, and then when I saw you sit down I thought I'd come over; no point us both sitting on our own. You *are* on your own?"

He sees her struck with a moment of doubt, suddenly worried she may have been intruding. "This morning I am. My usual canteen partner didn't make it into work."

"Oh?"

"Nothing untoward I'm sure. He was working on an important textbook over the weekend — there was a deadline — and so they've probably given him today off instead."

"That makes sense." Momentarily she glances down from his face to his shirt. "Did you buy a new tie?"

"A tie?"

"Yes. On Friday you told me you were shopping for a new tie. When we met in the café."

"Did I tell you that?"

She nods.

"Well I'm afraid I didn't. It was a wasted trip."

"That's a shame." She pauses just an instant, allowing the background hum to intrude for a moment. "They didn't have any?"

"No, it wasn't that. The shop had some, but not as many as they used too — and just about all of them were blue." Vincent glances around the room, trying to focus on the men; without exception they are wearing ties, and these are nearly all blue. Here and there is a hint of colour, but from the shape and style of those he can tell they are very old. He looks back to Marina; she seems to be expecting more from him. "And not just the ties. Shirts, jackets, trousers; very limited choice all of a sudden."

Marina lifts her cup to her lips. "That must have been frustrating."

"Frustrating? I don't know. I was a little bit annoyed, I'll admit that much." Vincent tries to recall his reaction.

"And confused too. I don't understand why there's suddenly so little choice."

Marina takes her turn to glance around the refectory. "Don't you think it looks smart, professional, the way people dress? Isn't there something in uniformity that suggests — I don't know — a common goal, a common purpose?"

He follows her eyes for a moment then, returning his gaze to her, finds she is looking at him intently.

"I don't mean to pry," she says. "I'm just interested. Being a woman it's slightly different of course, though we too have our norms."

Vincent remembers the second thing that had bothered him about his shopping expedition.

"So — being a woman — have you also found that things have suddenly got really expensive?"

"'Things'?"

"Like shoes. I noticed how expensive shoes and boots had become — not that I was shopping for any, you understand. And books too! That was a real surprise."

She laughs. "When was the last time you shopped?"

Vincent looks sheepish. "A while I suppose."

"And what about food, and everyday staples?"

"Like most people I have mine delivered, the money taken straight from my salary by the Ministry."

"I thought so." She raises her mug again. "Well, if you'd been paying attention — and how like a man not to! — you would have noticed that everything has gradually been getting more expensive. It always does, doesn't it? But if you go looking for boots once every year then you're bound to notice the difference in price, aren't you?"

He feels as if he has just been lectured. "I suppose so."

"You didn't wonder" — and here she lowered her voice just a little — "whether there was something 'wrong'…" Her question trails away, partly formed.

Vincent wonders what he had thought. Hadn't he merely been surprised? Surely it was no more than that.

"No. Of course not."

✻

"I'm afraid I have some disturbing news." It is the afternoon and Verna is standing at the head of the Common Room delivering the weekly team update. It is a ritual with which few people actually engage, a repetitive round of Ministry messages, departmental updates, and so forth. But to begin as she does immediately suggests something different. "It's about Noah."

There is something theatrical about her delivery, as if the administration of a coup de grâce. Everyone is suddenly paying attention.

"Is he unwell?" comes a voice from the back — though no-one turns to see who has spoken. All eyes are fixed on Verna, looking for a response.

"He has been arrested," she says, knowing flatness of delivery will only heighten its impact.

"Arrested! What for?" Another semi-anonymous voice asks the obvious question. This time Verna scans the back of the room to identify the speaker.

"Sedition." Another bland punch. "After a long and not insignificant investigation it has been discovered that during his time in fiction he was planting his own ideas into the novels on which he worked, surreptitiously making suggestions, accusations against the Ministry, our work here."

"But that's treason." The first voice from the back of the room again. "If found guilty…"

"Indeed," Verna wastes no time, "and at the moment — based on what I have been told — things do not stand well with him. In fact the evidence seems overwhelming, and they expect a verdict within days. Which can only mean…" She allows her own voice to trail away, then strafes the room with her eyes.

She settles on Vincent.

"You took over from him, Vincent. He never gave you any indication as to what he had been up to? No clue? No" — a brief pause — "instruction?"

He reddens slightly at being singled out, even if he understands why she has done so.

"Nothing. Nothing at all. I'm stunned." Yet even as he utters the words he isn't sure he believes them. There has always been something slightly odd about Noah. "We never worked on the same books. I mean, he didn't hand over anything to me that needed finishing." It is the answer to a question he hasn't been asked. He is conscious of the colour in his face.

"Exactly according to protocol. And I'm sure if he had tried to 'involve' you in some way, you would have reported it."

"Yes, of course."

If his statement is untrue it is not that he *wouldn't* have reported Noah, but rather the result of a sudden and disturbing notion that he couldn't be certain as to what he *would* have done.

Verna's gaze releases him and returns to the rest of the room.

"This is, of course, another reminder of the vital work we do, the important role we play. Ours is a great responsibility, to look after and protect all those who read the books we work on. But it is a burden too, one that can weigh heavily on the weak," her eyes are back to Vincent, "or the misguided." She pauses, almost as if she expects to be prompted, then answers a question no-one has asked. "Our last such case was nine years ago. I know this would have been before some of you started working here, but you will probably have heard of Marcus F." A few nods. "Although I was new here myself, I met Marcus. He was a charming and erudite man, full to the brim with knowledge and brilliance. Yet he was also tainted with revolutionary thoughts, corrupted by ideas from some of the old texts, the pre-Ministry books. Being in his presence was — quite frankly — dangerous for the young and impressionable. Noah knew him, though until recently it was assumed only tangentially. And there were others who might have fallen under his spell had he not been apprehended."

The silence that follows contains the rest of the warning Verna needs to deliver. Then she moves on to more mundane matters.

Immediately abstracted, Vincent recalls how Noah had spoken of Marcus in hushed tones, talked him through the events when they came and removed him from the office. It had been pure theatre; deliberately so. What Vincent hadn't told Noah in reply — indeed, had told no-one — was that he too had met Marcus.

❋

"It was a shame about your friend."

Citing the need to visit an ailing uncle further along the 10's route, Marina had found him waiting at the tram stop after work. She makes her statement a few minutes later, just as they are passing the Botanical Gardens.

"I'm sure it's a mistake. They haven't convicted him yet," Vincent replies.

"Who's that?" She seems perplexed.

"Noah."

She shakes her head. "Who's Noah? Anyway, I didn't mean him, whoever he is. I meant Marcus."

"Marcus?"

"That was his name, wasn't it?" She is thrown by Vincent's confusion.

"But that was years ago!" He tries to humour her. "And before I started work at the Ministry. On that basis I don't see how you could imagine he was my friend — or where that notion might have sprung from."

She places a hand on his arm. "I'm sorry; I must have got mixed-up. Perhaps someone said something to me about this 'Noah' and I misunderstood. It's the most likely scenario, isn't it? I didn't mean to imply anything. Or to make any kind of accusation. We've only just met and now I've offended you. Will you forgive me?"

And how can he not, especially with her holding onto his arm, the tram rocking slightly side-to-side, the novelty of the whole experience undermining him?

"Let me make you dinner — next weekend — to make up for my clumsiness."

*

It had been during a career fair held early in his final year at college. A raft of professionals paraded before them over a two-day period, each extolling the virtues of the industry in which they worked, the jobs they did, the positive impact their efforts had on the general populous. Vincent and his cohort learned about heavy industry and light industry, health-care, transportation. Nearly half the presenters were either Ministry employees or worked in companies with Ministry ties — though none of that was a surprise to the young people being bombarded with information.

Punch-drunk, audiences dwindled during the second afternoon either because the students had been to the sessions of greatest interest to them, or — keen to escape — pretended to have done so. Vincent was still searching for something undefined however, not that he expected anything positive to come from the final presentation of the day.

There were only three of them left in the auditorium when Marcus entered, a situation which didn't seem to bother him at all. Ushering them down to the front, he pulled together an arc of three chairs and one for himself, asked their names, what they were studying, and whether they had any firm ideas as to their next career step. Vincent had been the only one who didn't have a clue. In spite of what the other two said, he knew they were both engineering-types and were just slugging through the day before they could go home.

"I expect when I describe my job to you it will sound the dullest thing in the world — but I assure you it is far from that. It has be the most exciting, the most stimulating, the most influential one."

That was how Marcus began, and yet there was nothing much in the mechanics of what he did, the processes themselves, to get the blood pumping. Then having spent fifteen minutes on the mundane, he changed tack.

"Now; it's not what we keep out of a book that counts, but what we might put in." Vincent had been struck that Marcus had chosen to frame it that way. He continued: "Take fiction, stories. Made-up things: made-up people, made-up worlds and so forth. The people living in those worlds have lives to live — just like we do — and in those lives they have to wrestle with important issues: politics, sex, religion."

The subjects he listed were semi-taboo, so much so that, when he spent the next ten minutes talking about each in turn, even the engineers were enthralled. Using real examples from their collective culture and history —

topics about which they would rarely hear anyone speak freely — Marcus drew on one or two incidents ('mythological incidents' he called them) to describe how an author might weave 'messages' into a story about fictional people in their fictional world. Vincent was struck by the approach: Marcus was explaining how the responsibility to eradicate subversion in books could only be met if one knew how the heresies might be successfully *included* in the first place: "you have to know how the wrong-doers work to circumvent the rules in order to be able to root their messages out. It's like literary hacking."

"If you can do all that you must be very good at your job," one of the engineers said, evidently impressed.

"Thank you," Marcus replied, "I like to think so."

At the end of the session, Vincent had been last to leave.

"Was that useful?" Marcus had called after him as he was walking toward the exit.

"Yes, thank you. Fascinating."

"And might it be something you would have an interest in, or consider pursuing?"

"Yes, it might." Vincent was unable to deny the attraction.

"In that case," Marcus had walked towards him and presented him with his Ministry business card. "We're always on the look-out for intelligent young people. If you've any questions or if there's anything I can help you with, just get in touch."

✻

The following Monday Verna calls Vincent into her office.

"Is there any news?" he asks, assuming she wants to talk to him about Noah. There seems to be a general consensus that he is the closest person to a friend Noah has at work.

"News?"

"About Noah?"

"Ah." Verna glances at her computer monitor. "This afternoon."

"'This afternoon' what?"

"The final verdict. Ratification, if you like." She allows a frown to form as if silently posing a follow-on question; or anticipating his own, perhaps.

"So they've already decided?"

"Occasionally such decisions are subject to validation, double-checking. Good practice, don't you think?"

Vincent chooses not to respond. Nor does he seek clarification on what verdict has been reached. Whether 'just' or not he has no idea, though an immediate feeling of unfairness arises from his inability to understand whether what Noah had supposedly done was heinous enough for him to face the ultimate sanction. From Vincent's perspective, Noah is little more than a blabber-mouth, a chatter-box, someone who likes the sound of his own voice. Surely he lacks the depth, the seriousness, to be a potent weapon of insurrection. Vincent can remember the very public dissection of Marcus F's life both before and after his execution: the litany of things he was supposed to have done, the corruptions for which he was allegedly responsible. Would they now do the same for Noah? Guilty or not, surely he is small fry in comparison.

"And what about you, Vincent?"

Verna's question pulls him from his brief reverie.

"Me?"

"You've been quiet of late. We wondered whether or not you had been adversely affected by the news about Noah. Upset, you know? Discomforted somehow…"

"Upset?" Vincent considers the idea for a moment — as well as trying to decipher who Verna might have meant by 'we'. "Yes, I suppose a little, just like everyone else. It was a shock, of course. Even though you don't really know someone that well, you're still surprised. Isn't that inevitable? He has always seemed — I don't know — harmless."

A small but sympathetic smile briefly appears on Verna's face and then is gone.

"That's an essential part of the act, don't you think? Such people — those who seek to undermine the order of things — are hardly likely to go shouting about it from the rooftops. They might appear exemplars for the way things are. Or then again they might choose to make so much noise, be so obvious, that they avoid suspicion. In Noah's case…well, I probably shouldn't tell you this, but we'd had our suspicions for some considerable time. There were plenty of clues. So please don't think any of this was hasty or careless. There was hard evidence. The Ministry wouldn't have acted without evidence."

"Yes, I suppose so."

A brief pause.

"As long as you're okay." It is a sign that the interview is over. Vincent rises. "And if you ever needed to talk…"

Vincent nods almost imperceptibly; tries a smile.

"Of course. Thank you. And I'm fine. Really."

❊

Whether or not Vincent needed to talk, there are now two people suddenly offering themselves up for the role. Verna is just doing her job, but Marina seems determined to engage him in a way that is a rarity for him — and all on the basis of an inconsequential coming together in a small and quaint café. Yet it is somehow more than that. As he sits at his desk throughout the remainder of the week he occasionally speculates as to what might come of their up-coming dinner engagement.

Aware only of the vague location of her unwell uncle, Vincent has no idea where she lives; yet he finds himself looking out for her when he gets on the tram to go to work in the morning and while waiting for the tram to go home at the end of the day. In the second half of the week he takes an extra coffee break both morning and afternoon, spends slightly longer than perhaps he should in the canteen, and all on the off-chance that he might see her — or that she might seek him out. Doing so is, he knows, distracting him from his work, and probably adding to Verna's suspicion that all is not well. And in a strange way, that is how it feels. He is slightly unnerved, off-balance; the news about Noah, Verna's intervention, and the mystery of Marina, all combine to confuse him.

As he travels home on Thursday evening a little later than usual, he mulls over his disquiet and finds himself adding to it, his experience when out shopping and his sudden recollection of meeting Marcus — his *first* meeting with Marcus — increasing the forces ranged against his equilibrium.

The arrival of a note in the internal mail mid-way through Friday morning does nothing to help re-ground him. Although it merely informs him of the time she will arrive at his house the following day (around five-thirty, in order to give her time to prepare their meal so they can eat around seven), it is sufficient to prompt a number of fresh questions — and to trigger another extended coffee break in the hope that he might see her in order to answer some of them. How, for example, has she acquired his address? He has not told her, of that he is sure. Perhaps if she knew someone who worked in the Personnel Department; well, it wouldn't be too hard to find it out. And what is she planning to cook? There were some things he didn't like; mushrooms, for example. And does he need to secure anything himself, an ingredient or a bottle of wine perhaps — even if the latter has recently become so much more expensive? Yet he knows these are essentially minor questions. As he steps down from the tram, larger ones remain; questions known but unarticulated.

*

Frank spreads the newspaper out on the kitchen table.

"Dear Sirs," he reads, "I feel compelled to offer my congratulations and thanks to the Government in relation to

their recent homelessness initiative. The people who have been littering our streets with their filthy boxes and bags can only be detrimental to the overall well-being of our society, not to mention doing themselves no good at all. I understand that a few will be true hard luck cases, but I suspect the majority are addicts, criminals, or simply too lazy to work. We have been pandering to the few at a cost to the many for far too long, and the new programme you have introduced in terms of Community Work Places seems to me the perfect antidote for all concerned."

He takes off his glasses and lays them on the paper, then looks up to where Deirdre is cleaning dishes at the sink.

"What do you think?" he asks.

"About what?"

"My letter." He is frustrated that she hasn't stopped what she is doing in order to listen to his reading. "In the paper."

At this Deirdre drops her hands to her side and turns. "What do you want me to say?"

"What you think, of course. About the letter."

"I can see why they published it," she says, then turns her back on him again.

"Which means?"

"That you've written what they wanted someone to write, that's all. You've articulated what most people are thinking; justified the Government's actions."

Frank is unsure what to do with her comment so puts a positive spin on it. "Well then; that's exactly what I was trying to do."

"And you believe it?" Again from over her shoulder.

"Believe what?"

"What you've written."

"Why shouldn't I?"

Vincent glanced up from the book to where Marcus was sitting at the other end of the park bench.

"What do you think?" Marcus asked.

"About this?" Vincent looked back at the highlighted passage unsure what kind of critique the older man was expecting. He had asked to meet Marcus again because there were some elements of the controller's job about which he wanted clarification, yet seemed to have found himself in an impromptu exam.

Marcus nodded.

"It's well-written, I suppose; a simple domestic scene. Nothing remarkable in that. Entirely believable, as I'm sure such things happen. I doubt the relationship between husband and wife is entirely harmonious."

"All true, but largely superficial." Marcus was smiling. "But from a controller's perspective; would there be anything there about which to be concerned?"

Vincent skimmed the passage again. "I don't think so. It all seems perfectly banal."

At this Marcus laughed loudly, and the younger man was forced to glance across the park to see if there was anyone nearby who might have been attracted by the sound. Apart from a few people near the fountain at the far gates, the two men had this particular corner to themselves.

"It's a superb piece of writing," Marcus slipped into mentor-mode, "and an absolute minefield for a controller." He paused long enough to slide closer, then took the book from him, pointing to the text as he spoke. "You're right in that it's a normal domestic scene; perfectly believable, as you say. But it tells us so much; not only that there was an issue with homelessness, but also the general public's view on it — i.e. Frank's view — as well as an indication as to the Government's theoretical actions. 'Theoretical', mind. The homeless are shirkers; that's what Frank is saying and what the novel tells us most people believed. But the Government's policy — in this work of fiction remember — although couched in benevolence, is essentially forced labour."

"But it doesn't say that," Vincent protested.

"Of course it doesn't; not explicitly. And if it did, we might have to cut it out." He pointed at the exchange with Deidre. "This is where we find out. You're right that there's tension there, and we not unnaturally assume it's merely domestic: she doesn't stop what she's doing so that she can listen to him; she's somewhat dismissive about his letter; and she doesn't agree with him. Oh, she may not say as much, but it's all there. 'And you believe it?' she says — because *she* doesn't. That's where the writing is clever; it shows us Frank as a puppet who can't think for himself and, through Deidre, suggests there might be an alternative view — and one the reader might want to consider for themselves."

Vincent took the book back and examined the words again. "But it didn't get edited out."

"No, it didn't."

"Why not?"

"Because it's a good piece of writing; not just technically, but because it has layers of meaning — layers that most people wouldn't get. And that's partly because people tend not to read thoroughly. Their reaction, their normal reaction, would be like yours: Deidre hates her husband, end of story."

Getting a clue from the way Marcus had spoken, Vincent's next question was one he might have posed earlier. "Did you work on this?"

"I did."

"But *you* saw those other things. Shouldn't you have done something about them?"

"Cut them out, you mean?"

Vincent nodded.

"And ruin a perfectly accurate domestic scene?" Marcus laughed again.

"But the controller's job…"

"Indeed, the controller's job. But there is also the role of the citizen too, don't you think? And there is *always* a different take on things, an alternative viewpoint. Who am I to stifle that — especially in a work of fiction?" Marcus paused, taking the book back and closing it. "One of the greatest skills a controller has to have isn't to know what needs to be cut out, but to understand what needs to be left in. You may discover that for yourself one day."

❋

On edge for most of the afternoon, when Marina arrives a little after five Vincent is unsure whether her finally being there eases or heightens the apprehension he has been feeling. He had spent the morning doing his laundry, then walked to the local shop in order to buy another over-priced bottle of wine, concerned that she might prefer red to the white he had already procured. He knows little about wine, and in the end made his choice based on a grape variety of which he had heard, and on the wine's strength, just under ten percent. A few years previously he had worked on a book about the history of western Europe, a potted version of events in France, Germany, Spain and elsewhere from the eighteenth to the end of the last century. All were wine-producing countries, and the book had contained a small addendum contrasting their viniculture. Vincent knows, therefore, that good wines used to boast strengths around thirteen percent, and that the best were from a single variety of grape. Such wines are still available he believes, but they are only within reach of the very few — the rich and the powerful. The red wine he eventually took home was of dubious vintage and obscure origin.

Marina had breezed into the house, accepted the very quick tour of the downstairs rooms (essentially just a lounge, a toilet, a walk-in cupboard, and the kitchen), and then set to work. Placing the two bags she brought with her onto the work-surface (and some of their contents into Vincent's small fridge), she seeks out a frying pan and two saucepans, and — as she puts it — "your best knife". She is cooking a pasta dish with chicken, and has assumed he would be fine with that. He tells her has a white wine as an accompaniment. Both proposals are acceptable; it is as if they have negotiated some kind of trade deal.

For the best part of an hour Vincent sits at the small kitchen table ostensibly reading, yet all the while watches Marina as she works. Evidently using the smaller of the two saucepans to prepare the sauce, he finds himself mesmerised by the way in which she tackles its components: the onion chopped into small precise pieces, the garlic expertly diced until it appears more like a paste than anything else. She is exact with her measurements of ingredients too, particularly spices. On the whole, it is an operation unlike anything he had ever seen. And all the while she has been happy to maintain a low-key dialogue with him. She asks about where he was born, his childhood, his education; and he furnishes her with suitably detailed answers, almost as if that is the price he has agreed to pay for her cooking their meal. When he tries a similar tack to establish something about her, she is subtly evasive, and while seeming to answer his questions manages to leave him with the sense that he hasn't uncovered very much at all. Perhaps discovering that she lives on the other side of town, somewhere near the zoo, is his most concrete find — but even then that is little more than a guess based on the number of a tram line.

"Sorry about your friend," she says, filling a slightly longer silence a little after six-twenty, stirring the sauce as she does so. Vincent looks up from his book. It is the second time she has made such a comment. "From your department."

"Noah? I didn't think it was public knowledge outside of our team."

"You're right, it isn't." She pauses to put some heat under the water-filled large saucepan. "It's just that I know someone in the communications department and occasionally he tells me what's coming up in the next staff briefing. He knew I was coming to see you — I told him where you worked and that you'd mentioned 'Noah' the last time we spoke — and he put two and two together, as they say."

"Isn't that, I don't know, dangerous?"

Marina laughs as if that is the most ridiculous thing she has ever heard. "Of course not! He knows he can trust me. And anyway, if I betrayed his confidence then I would be in just as much trouble wouldn't I?"

"And now you've told me."

She laughs again. "Don't be silly! Now set the table, I'm going to heat the pasta soon."

Vincent does as he's told, putting out plates and coasters, cutlery and glasses, as if it is the most natural thing in the world for him to do — and not at all as if he had practiced earlier that afternoon.

A little before seven Marina serves the pasta and chicken sauce, and they sit down to eat. Vincent offers a toast in thanks; she laughs again. Every time she does so she appears younger, and he struggles again — as he has struggled ever since he met her — to assign her an age.

The food is delicious.

"Where did you learn to cook like this?" he asks.

"At home, when I was younger." She puts down her fork and picks up her glass. "We lived on a small farm out in the country. Most of the time it was just my mother, my two sisters, and me. My father was away quite a lot of the time; he worked for the Ministry. We had chickens mainly; a few pigs; very small crops of vegetables. Just what the four of us girls could practically manage. It was a limited palette, so we had to be inventive with our cooking in order to avoid boredom. And then my mother introduced a competitive element to proceedings."

"'Competitive element'? What do you mean?"

"As soon as we were all old enough, she had my sisters and I each cook once a week. It was, she said, good practice for the future. And it spurred us on to try things out, for our meal to be better than the others'." Marina takes a sip of wine then puts her glass back on the table.

"Were you the best?"

Another laugh. "I like to think so!" She looks at her plate as she spears a piece of chicken. "This was always one of my favourites."

"I've never had anything like it," Vincent confesses. "And I mean that in a good way!"

The food and the laughter having relaxed them, he feels himself on more solid ground.

"And then you left the farm and came to the city?"

She scoops up some more pasta. "Yes. My father got me a job in the Ministry." She stops briefly. "No, that sounds like something it isn't. He got me an introduction, an interview. *I* got the job. Very low-level, of course; menial admin work. I've moved on a little since then."

"Does he still work there, your father?"

She shakes her head. "Semi-retired; I think that's how you'd describe him."

"What did he do?" As soon as the words are out, Vincent knows he has crossed a line. It is not the sort of question you asked, prying into the roles of Ministry employees. He backtracks. "No, don't tell me. I don't need to know. I'm an idiot. And you probably can't tell me anyway."

Having taken the last of the chicken from her plate, Marina smiles. "Shall we go and sit in the other room? We can wash-up later."

They spend the next half an hour sitting side-by-side on the sofa, their conversation meandering through innocuous topics: favourite parts of the city; favourite tram line; most inspiring books they have read; the best book Vincent has worked on — and then the most difficult. She seems intrigued as to the process he goes through when tackling a text, what he has to look for; and in fiction, how he makes his choices as to what he edits out or leaves in. These are, he assumes, questions of an avid reader, and so he is happy that she seems interested, that the focus is on him. As he downs the last of the wine, he wonders what he had been so nervous about.

"Would you like some coffee?" he asks, making to get up.

Her hand on his arm stays him.

"Am I forgiven?" she asks.

"For what?"

"If you remember, I'm here as a kind of penance, payment for intruding into your life so suddenly and so clumsily."

He smiles. "Nothing to forgive. I'm glad you're here."

There is a moment where neither of them move. The house is eerily silent as if all sound has been sucked from it. Had you been in the lounge and stood by the window, you might have heard a tram rattling two streets away, or the quiet conversation of two people walking the pavement outside. In a nearby tree an owl hoots.

But Vincent hears none of that, transfixed as he watches Marina's hand move from his arm up to his chest. Once there, her fingers undo one of his shirt buttons. Returning his gaze to her face, he finds her intent on his eyes, her hand moving by feel alone. As he searches for a clue, he feels a frown begin to build — only for it to be chased away by the beginning of a smile on her lips. Raising his own hands, he places them on her shoulders, watching all the time for instruction, permission. And then he moves them to her blouse, begins to undo the buttons there, and when they are all loosed, peels back her shirt to reveal her white bra, her slightly freckled chest.

She leans back on to sofa and pulls him towards her. They kiss. Hesitant at first, he is intoxicated by her confidence as her tongue explores his, and for a few minutes is completely lost. Then she eases him away, arches her back, allows his hands to find the clasp of her bra. Once undone, he slips the straps from her shoulders and drops the bra to the floor. Her breasts are shapely rather than large, her nipples — only slightly darker than her skin — small but proud. He bends his head to them; gathers them, each in turn, into his mouth; licks them with his tongue; caresses the mounds of her breasts with his hands. And all the while she lays back, her head now bent slightly away from him, her hands on the back of his head, in his hair.

After a minute or so he pushes himself away from her.

"Wow," he says. She is still smiling.

"Forgiven then," she jokes, and pulls him into another kiss.

They remain locked like that for a little longer until, lifting himself up again, he watches his own hands as they run down from her breasts onto her belly and from there to the button in the waistband of her trousers. As he begins to release it, Marina's hand lands on his, envelops his fingers, stills them.

"I don't think so, do you?"

And with those words the spell is broken.

Sitting a little more upright, the Marina reclining before him suddenly seems like a different person, as if the one who had been there just moments previously was banished with those words. He feels a frown forming again — one she does nothing to chase away.

"I need to be getting back," she says, a tone of apology in her voice. "My last tram is in less than an hour and we need to wash up; and I need to get my things together."

"You could…" he begins, but is immediately unsure what she could or could not do. Indeed, he has no idea about himself either. "I…" But it is another unfinished, inadequate sentence.

"I know," she says, smiling again as she retrieves her bra from the floor and, with a dexterity that surprises him, puts it on in what seems like an instant.

Vincent cannot help but stare at the soft material of the bra cups as if the flesh they cradle is nothing more than something mythological he once read about in a book.

She pecks him on the cheek as she stands — "I'll wash, you dry" — and is suddenly gone from the room.

❋

Beyond the Ministry's light and airy public spaces, the building is rapidly transformed into a rabbit warren of passageways and rooms; the further you are from the main atrium, the smaller the spaces become. Towards the rear of the building, at the end of a narrow and nondescript first floor corridor, a fire-door opens out onto a metal stairway which leads down to a small private carpark.

Although it is uncommon for the building to be occupied at the weekend (except for the twenty-four hour service and security functions) this Sunday afternoon the lights are burning inside 1.51, the last room before the fire escape. A point for emergency egress, on this occasion it has been unlocked and used as a point of entry. At the foot of the steps, two cars wait in the early evening darkness.

Four people sit around the room's rectangular meeting table. On one side are two men — one bearded and clearly senior to his clean-shaven colleague both in terms of age and rank — and opposite them two slightly younger women. There is a similar age difference between the men and the women, perhaps ten or fifteen years. The older of the women is Verna.

"He said nothing useful?" The bearded man asks his younger male counterpart.

"Nothing of any real value, no. You must understand — as I know you do — at that stage he would have said absolutely anything in order to save himself; confessed to anything; implicated anyone. In the final interview he was raving really. That and bursting into tears."

The older man looks toward Verna. "Does that sound about right?"

"Yes — except the crying part." Verna glances down at the table as if she is expecting to find some papers there to which she can refer, something she has brought from her office perhaps. But the table-top is bare. "He was talking all the time. Couldn't help himself. Liked the sound of his own voice I suppose."

"A distraction tactic," the younger man suggests. "Common enough practice. Gives the notion that you're not particularly competent. A disguise to throw you off the scent."

"And was he?" The older man to Verna again.

"Competent?" she weighs up her answer. "Reasonably so. Or at least, he wasn't incompetent. His work was of an adequate standard: not particularly quick; reasonably accurate."

"There would have been an instance or other — presumably triggered by a check of some sort — which led to him being moved him out of fiction."

Verna nods. "I know you've read the reports; that you're familiar with the case. After all, getting approval…"

"Certainly." The younger man butts in. "Yet it was a long process in the end, wasn't it? Nearly two years. Enough time to act on suspicions."

"Or for suspicions to be confirmed," suggests the senior man. He stands and walks to the small window where he pauses, runs his fingers across his beard, and looks down into the carpark. "No-one is suggesting you have done anything wrong, Verna." He turns and smiles. He is close enough to put a reassuring hand on her shoulder, though he does not. "In fact the opposite. You gave him plenty of time to get comfortable, confident; for him to think he was safe; for evidence to be compiled."

"Do you think it is inconclusive?"

The other three look at the younger man; the tension in the room increases a notch. It is as if he is challenging them to denigrate his contribution to their work.

The older man returns to his seat. "I know what you mean, Will. And it's always difficult isn't it — unless there are extenuating circumstances. I *have* read the reports of course, and I would say the case was" — he pauses to find the word he needs — "marginal. As they can be, of course. But then once challenged… Well, he hardly helped himself with his blabbing making it difficult to tell what was true and what not. And we have to recognise that, on occasion, it can be necessary to make — a sacrifice." Another pause for the mot juste. "For the greater good. For protection. To prove to the people who matter that we're on top of things; to continue to convince them that the order which governs all our lives is safe and secure with us." He looks at the other three in turn, almost as if he is asking them to deny what he has said.

"He would have confessed to anything," Will repeats after a few moments, as if that were the seal on something and the only statement needed to bring the matter to a satisfactory conclusion. Had there been some papers on the table, they might have signed them then and there, confirmed their judgement, set final wheels in motion, then escaped down into the carpark and the early evening.

"And his colleagues?" The bearded man to Verna again. "There is one you're interested in. One with 'potential'?"

"Vincent, yes."

"Did Noah mention him — explicitly, I mean?"

"In the interrogation he mentioned a number of people by name," Will speaks before Verna is able to, as if trying to impress, "and Vincent was one of them. But there was nothing tangible."

"Verna?"

"I have to say that he never talked to me about anyone other than himself. Of course, when we had departmental moves and things like that he might make a comment; lots of people did. And when Vincent took over from him in fiction there would have been the odd conversation about how he was getting on — Vincent, I mean. But Noah was always focussed on himself."

"The self-centred can be the most dangerous," Will volunteers. "There is no greater cause than themselves."

"Or no better disguise," the older man suggests. He pauses, his eyes on Will for a heartbeat longer than necessary. "And from what you say, Vincent is an almost exact opposite: quiet, thorough, diligent. In some respects an exemplary employee."

"In many respects, undoubtedly."

"Yet there's a trace of doubt in your voice, Verna."

Looking down to where her hands rest on the table, Verna wishes she had something for her fingers to be busy with, or a pen with which to take notes — even though she knows note-taking in sessions such as this is not permitted.

"It's difficult to say exactly why — especially with someone who is so naturally quiet and reserved. But I have been getting an increasing sense of disquiet from him, as if there is something bothering him or bubbling away beneath the surface, whether he realises it or not. It was one of the reasons I spoke individually to him about Noah."

"You wanted to test his reaction?" Will voices his approval, offers a slight nod.

"And?"

"He seemed shocked. Just what you would expect when you discover a colleague has been found to be... I'm never sure of the appropriate word these days." It is a statement accompanied by a nervous laugh.

The senior man nods. "Of course. But there was nothing in Vincent's shock to suggest that he was aware of what Noah was alleged to be engaged in? No sign of a guard slipping?"

"Nothing."

"Which could mean a number of things of course; anything from extreme guilt to extreme innocence. The potential for action, or the certainty of inaction." He turns to the younger woman. "What else do we know?"

"Exactly as Verna says: he's a quiet, reserved person; lives alone in a small house; no evidence of a significant other — at least not in the recent past. He likes his routine; doesn't have any obvious interests outside of work — which he clearly takes pride in, and for which he was probably always going to be a good fit."

The older man acknowledges something unspoken. "And the Ministry? What does he think about us?"

"That's harder to say, don't you think, Verna?" A nod of confirmation. "He appears to understand his purpose, what the department is trying to do. As I say, I think he's a creature of habit, uncomfortable with change."

"Verna?"

"I'd agree with all that. I've never had any significant sense of resentment."

"Though there is one small thing." The other three turn to the younger woman again. "He wanted to buy a tie the other day — one that wasn't blue — and was unable to find one. That surprised him, I think; knocked him back a little bit. Change, like I said. And the prices of boots. The fact that they have gone up so much. He knows the Ministry is responsible, but…"

"Such minor things!" Will laughs. "Surely not enough to use as evidence for of leaning one way or the other."

"You'd be surprised how large and fast a tree can grow from even the smallest acorns, Will."

*

They were back on the same park bench a week later.

"So you're seriously thinking about applying for the controllers' department?"

"I'm interested, yes."

Marcus smiled. "And what is it that appeals to you?"

"The type of work." Vincent paused for a moment. "I'm quite a methodical person; I like detail. Perhaps I have a forensic mind."

"'Forensic'; that's quite a word!" They both laughed. "Anything else apart from the nature of the work? For example, how would you describe your relationship with books and with people?"

"I like books." Vincent stalled. He had never before considered the possibility of having a 'relationship' with anything inanimate. "I have more books than the average person, I suppose — and I doubt I could ever have enough. And I've quite eclectic tastes." He laughed at the vague hollowness of his claims, as if he was trying to impress in an interview. "That makes it sound as if I've a huge study at home, but it's really only a bookcase. And I use the public library a fair bit."

"Which is all very promising — though you'll be pleased to know that having a vast private library at home isn't a prerequisite for the job! The rest of course — having eclectic tastes and so forth — is much more relevant." Marcus's smile was intended to be supportive and encouraging. It seemed to be doing its job. "And what about people?"

This was a much harder question to answer. An only child, his parents had not been gregarious and outgoing, so his upbringing had been low-key, modest, almost reclusive.

"I find people a challenge sometimes." Vincent could see no point in lying, if only because he was sure Marcus had already deconstructed him perfectly adequately. "And I don't necessarily mean the flesh-and-blood of people."

"Is there any other kind?"

"I think so, don't you? The person who sits below the surface or beneath the facade. The private person, the real person with their secrets and beliefs."

"Their unspoken lives?" Marcus suggested, clearly interested.

"Yes! What a great way to put it, 'their unspoken lives'…"

"And so books…"

Vincent knew Marcus was leading him on — and he was happy to be led.

"Books speak to *that* person, not the flesh-and-blood one. I suppose that's another reason why what you do is interesting to me: to communicate at some vital level."

"And — if I may be so bold — not merely that, but to communicate what's important." Marcus thought for a moment, even though familiar with his theme. "Books talk to the inner person, the secret person; they can make direct contact with all those subterranean feelings and desires you speak of. Books touch us — especially fiction, because through fiction we can live different lives, better lives, lives not limited by how pretty things are or how fast we run or how much we earn." He stopped himself and smiled apologetically. "Forgive me. I can get carried away."

"If you were trying to do a sales-job on me then it's working!"

They both laughed.

Vincent looked out across the park at the people there, walking, talking, holding their children near the edge of the fountain, feeding the fish that swam within its copious — if half-empty — reservoir.

"It is a job with two sides." Marcus's voice pulled Vincent back from his consideration of a young mother pushing a buggy. "The first is the technical side. You know, the 'how' of the work: how you process the words, check the grammar; how you re-sequence a badly written sentence; how you leave out the irrelevant, or enhance the relevant. These are the skills you can learn through reading, or by being taught."

"And the other side?"

"Much more nebulous." Again a pause. "This is the philosophical side, or the political, the emotional — all those things which centre on belief. Not the belief of the writer you understand — all of that is there in their words, the raw material the controller has to work with — but of the controller themselves... You remember what I said last week about deciding what to leave out? That relates exactly to the philosophical. It's driven by what *you* believe — because make no mistake Vincent, whether you think you do or not, everyone believes in something."

"What do you believe in?"

Marcus laughed. "If only it was that easy!" Another break, this time it was Marcus's turn to look out across the park, to include its visitors in his argument. "All those people have things they believe in, that drive them, that they are prepared to act on in order to protect, or achieve, or deny. And all of those things, that stimuli, is predicated on what I like to call 'neutrality'. Have you heard the term?"

"No, not in this context. What does it mean?"

"That you are either a neutral person or you are not. And not in terms of yourself — I think we have to assume that everyone is completely biased when it comes to themselves! — but in relation to society, the world around them. Take this park." He gestured towards the fountain. "There will be those who think this is just 'a park'; they walk it in, play in it, take it for granted. But there will be others who *care* about the park; who get upset if they see weeds out of control, or a bench vandalised, or a patch of bare earth where nothing has been planted. Such people are not neutral about the park because they would — theoretically — take action to make it better. And you can use the park as a metaphor for just about anything: our economic system, the local football team, the tram timetable, even the Ministry."

"The Ministry?"

"And books, Vincent. That's where belief can find a voice, an outlet; that's where you can speak to the souls of the people. The people who are not neutral." Marcus smiled to himself. "There I go, preaching again!"

"But that's perfect; thank you." Vincent attempted to conjure a question that would prove he had understood not only what Marcus said but how one might be impacted if you were a controller. "So are you saying that I need to understand whether or not I am 'neutral' — and if so, what am I not neutral about? And then, knowing that, come to understand how it might influence my work in the future?"

Marcus stood. "Precisely so. Controller or some other role in some other profession. You may not know it now of course — your neutrality, that is — but it will already be there buried within you, formed by your history and your vision of how the world could be." He held out his hand which Vincent rose to shake. "Let me know what you decide to do."

✳

"We need to wrap-up," says the older man. The conversation had meandered inconclusively for a few minutes. "We mentioned the idea of a test for Vincent.

Clearly we need to do something more to rule him 'in' or 'out'. Agreed." The other three nod. "So, unless anyone has any better ideas, I have a little experiment I'd like to try."

Verna sits a little further forward in her chair; the younger woman a little further back.

"Of course," says Will.

"I think we should give him a book to re-edit."

"Just that?" Verna seems surprised.

"Yes. Sounds too simple, doesn't it? But because of that he won't be suspicious or think it out of the ordinary."

"And the book?" asks Will.

"Again nothing contentious on the face of it. But it is a book he will remember. It is a book with, shall we say, 'connotations'. It will pose a significant challenge to him." Pulling a small notebook and a pen from his jacket pocket, the senior man tears out a sheet of paper. He writes down the title of a book and hands it to Verna.

She raises her eyebrows. "I don't think I know it."

Will takes the sheet from her, reads the title, then passes it back.

A few minutes later four figures descend the fire escape having locked both it and room 1.51 behind them. The older man and the younger woman get into one of the cars, Will into the other. And Verna begins her walk back to the tram stop hoping she will be in time to get the eight o'clock home.

They are part way to the suburbs when the young woman speaks. "Why will he know the book?"

"Because I introduced it to him before he became a controller. I had been giving a careers talk to some college students. It was the end of the day; only Vincent and two or three others turned up. Overall, an unremarkable event — except that Vincent asked to see me subsequently; said he had some questions about the job. We met a few times; at least twice, I think. There's a particular passage in that book I walked him through, so he knows what's in there, just beneath the surface."

"What *you* left in there," Marina points out, "although that was a younger version of you — and one without a beard."

"Yes." Marcus smiles slightly, his only recognition of her joke. "Which makes it a form of double-jeopardy for him. Firstly because he knows I was the one who originally edited the book and, as you say, knows what I failed to remove. Secondly, he has knowledge of my subsequent history — the false public history that can be tied to the book in only one way — which will no doubt weigh heavily too and add to the pressure. How he edits that passage will tell us a lot."

"Such as?"

"Whether or not he is neutral. What his leanings are. What he believes in, if anything. And, if he does have a bias, for which side — though I hate to be so binary, so reductive; that's Will's territory. If he leaves it as is — or even enhances it — that will tell us one thing; yet it will only take a few small changes to remove its sting, and if that's what he chooses to do then he will be telling us something else."

"And then we'll know."

"And then we'll have a better idea." For a moment Marcus watches the lights in the buildings as they make their way from the centre of town. "But what about you?"

"Me?"

"I didn't want to bring up your encounter with him, not in front of the others."

Marina frowns. "They don't know?"

"No. I daresay they'll assume you've done some digging in the background — it's your job after all — but that will have been the extent of your involvement. And because you're who you are... Well, they daren't question that." Slowing before a red light, Marcus brings the car to a halt. "You weren't in any danger or out of control?"

"At no point." She tries to sound as certain as she can, not wishing to be pressed.

"And" — interrupted by the lights changing to green, Marcus propels them forward once more — "you don't as a result feel any sympathy towards him? From what I recall he's a perfectly pleasant young man." He shoots her a glance then returns his eyes to the road.

"Yes he is. And neutral or not, he's definitely harmless in that way. But he's not really my type, dad." Marina allows a few hundred metres to pass. "So the meal and everything... It was just work, up to but not crossing a line; a favour for a parent..."

"Don't you dare tell your mother; she'd kill me!" They both laugh.

"To be honest, I'm not sure how much I found out that's of worth to you." She is distracted for a moment by a sudden wondering if she has learned anything new about herself. "Nor how much more there is to uncover; probably not very much without forcing him to commit to something. On that basis, is that the end of the experiment?" Marina's voice as flat and business-like as she can make it.

"Nearly." Marcus swings the car off the main road and through a set of gates. "I would just like you to give him something... We'll see what happens then."

*

Vincent's inclination is not to go to work on Monday. If he was to phone in and complain that he wasn't well he is certain they would take him seriously. How could there possibly be any suspicion? Indeed, Verna has already expressed concern that recently he 'hadn't been himself' — which he most certainly isn't the day after the meal.

He bumbles through Sunday on a vague form of autopilot, relying on habit and memory to get him through. Consequently he eats when he usually does, ensures he remains hydrated, watches too much television in spite of the limited selection on offer. Yet there are differences too; in the afternoon, a longer walk than usual in an attempt to clear the confusion from his head.

As he walks he takes himself through the previous evening in as much detail as he can manage, attempting to recall morsels of conversation, subtleties of looks and movement. It proves impossible not to focus on what happened in the lounge, a remembrance occluded by emotion — primarily guilt. Convinced he had done something wrong, as he ticks off laps of the park he tries to focus on the sequence of things and — a little like his circuitous walking — finds himself always returning to the same point: Marina had been the initiator. She had asked if she was forgiven, had played with his buttons, had lain back on the sofa, arched her back so that he might remove her bra, caress her breasts. What had he been doing in any of that other than be at her beck-and-call, following her lead, performing as expected? And then to be so suddenly rebuffed, dismissed.

Before Marina arrived he had been concerned with how he might survive her presence, and now he is faced with trying to understand how he can cope with her absence. It is as if a vital sentence had been edited from a book. Not having resolved that question — the nature of their relationship, or even whether or not they have one — part of his reluctance to go back to the Ministry is driven by not wanting to run into her in the canteen.

In the end the dilemma proves too difficult to resolve and so he allows his Monday morning routine to take over. Five hours further on and he is sitting with the rest of the department listening to Verna as she delivers the Ministry's weekly briefing. Although the formal — and final — news on Noah is perfunctory, it still manages to draw gasps from some members of the team. It is clear that at one point Verna chooses to embellish the script to provide a little more detail. Given he had been a member of her staff, Vincent thinks such a diversion is warranted, the least she can do. Yet what she delivers is hardly a rallying-cry (she isn't that kind of person), but rather an attempt to add a little humanity to the Ministry's cold words.

When she holds him back at the end of the meeting he is unsurprised; it seems a logical bookend to their previous conversation.

"How are you?"

"A little tired," he says. "I didn't sleep that well over the weekend."

"I'm not surprised," she confesses, and then chases the comment away with "thinking about Noah, I mean. Knowing the news would break today."

For a moment he says nothing. Then: "But I'm here now; back in harness as it were." He watches the phrase register with her, the look on her face suggesting a slightly different interpretation to that intended.

"That's what I wanted to talk to you about." Verna shuffles herself from one mode to another. "I've a new project for you."

"Oh?"

"You're just coming to the end of a book, aren't you?"

Though certain he is displaying some kind of confusion, he nods. His work-list has been set only recently and she has already given him a sequence of new novels to edit, work that will take him at least three months. To disrupt a plan so soon is highly unusual.

"There's a proposal to reissue some of our old titles. The Ministry recognises their worth as works of fiction but is concerned that times have changed, that the intervening years may not have been — what shall we say — kind to them?"

"They need updating?"

"Purely cosmetically. I'm sure that's what most of it is. But if a job's worth doing, and all that... After all, we'd hate to lose a good book because our readers found it old-fashioned or irrelevant."

He nods again.

Verna turns to the table behind her and removes a book which had been part-hidden under a pile of papers. "We thought we'd start with this."

Only half-way from her hands to his and Vincent has already recognised it. And he knows that within it he will find the section starting *'Frank spreads the newspaper out on the kitchen table'*.

❋

The next two and a half days pass unremarkably. Vincent allows the closing out of his existing project to drag on, wanting to put off Verna's new challenge for as long as possible. When on Wednesday afternoon she comes to see how he is getting on, his response — "just tidying up some loose ends; starting on the other book first thing tomorrow" — leaves him no further room for manoeuvre. On the tram home he tries to tell himself that Frank's story is just another book, just another job; that there is no reason for him to treat it any differently to all the other books on which he has worked. He has a proven process; surely all he needs to do is to trust in that?

When he arrives home and opens his front door he finds a card from the postal service waiting for him. It tells him they have been unable to deliver a parcel and instead left it with his neighbour who signed for it. Without bothering to remove his coat, Vincent walks back outside and heads to the adjacent house. The door opens just before he gets there. Mrs. Carsington has been waiting for him, watching through the curtains.

The package is not large; about half the width of a piece of paper, but the same length. Nor is it heavy. He places it on the kitchen table and eyes it warily as he removes his coat. He has ordered nothing, is expecting nothing. Hand-written, his name and address presents itself in clear and even script, blue ink. The postmark suggests its origin as being the centre of town, so neither that nor the handwriting provide any clue to the sender. The rear of the package is blank. Teasing at the tape, Vincent opens it carefully, peeling back the brown wrapping to reveal a long thin white card container inside. Flipping one end open, he allows his fingers to find the contents — tissue paper, without a doubt — which he then withdraws and lays on the table. Then he peels back the vibrant purple tissue.

A bright red tie.

Along with the tie is a small card, written in the same hand as on the front of the package: *I hope this is suitable, M.* He turns the card over expecting to find more words, an address perhaps; he checks the tissue paper and the package to ensure he has missed nothing. There is just the present and the card.

Vincent sits down to examine the tie. It is partially made from silk — which suggests expense. In terms of colour and style, it is exactly the kind of tie for which he had so recently shopped. And it is a tie which, had he found it, he would have wanted to buy but been unable to afford. *I hope this is suitable.* He looks at the words again and realises he has no idea what they mean, the heart of their message hidden beneath the blue ink. *Am I forgiven*, perhaps. Then he hears her voice: "I don't think so, do you?"

✳

As if I didn't have enough to worry about...

It is well beyond seven o'clock when he stops writing. Sitting at the kitchen table, still in his work clothes, Vincent realises he is hungry. Hungry and tired. Pulled from a drawer an hour earlier, the notebook, now closed and face-down before him, feels suddenly alien. As he looks at it he almost wonders how it has come to be laying there — and what it might contain. Yet he is well aware of its contents (if no longer the exact words themselves) and his instinct is to classify them; the controller in him wants to assign them a label. Knowing they are autobiographical, part of him wishes they weren't, a sliver that would like the notebook to contain nothing but fiction. Under such circumstances he could reopen the book and start editing, and through that process not only change what the words said but the past they laid bare too. And perhaps the future to which they pointed. It would be a way of coming to a resolution. Or of avoiding one. But he will not edit his words. No matter how much he might want to.

It is a small leap to wonder if, when addressing the novel he must pick up in the morning, his editing there might achieve something similar, to go back in time and alter the past. Even though Marcus talked him through just one short section, Vincent knows he will feel the older man's presence throughout the work; his touch on each page, on each sentence. When he tackles the passage with Frank and his wife in the kitchen, to what extent will he be peeling away the veneer of an encounter on a park bench and thus subtracting from or adding to *that*?

How is he supposed to know what to do?

"Trust the process" a voice says somewhere in his head. It is an amalgam of Marcus's voice, and Verna's, and Marina's. He imagines pausing with his fingers above a keyboard ready to strike and Marina saying "I don't think so, do you?" — and he wonders whether she will be right, and if so, whether he will listen.

Yet in a way it is neither the process nor the editing which will be tomorrow's problem; Vincent even wonders whether the words themselves might somehow prove superfluous. Surely what will count — in this instance perhaps more than any other in his experience — is meaning, the difference between what the words signify and the underlying dynamic of the message they convey. Frank is a model citizen; his wife may or may not be of an entirely different persuasion. Wasn't that what Marcus had been telling him all those years ago? What else had he been inferring, because there had been a message hidden in his spoken words too. That the author had written the politically disgruntled woman into the story and Marcus had chosen to leave her there, or that Marcus had shaped her that way himself? Vincent knows both are practically possible, the first requiring a blind eye, the second a degree of skill — and both belief. But as he realises this, he also sees even that is not at the heart of the issue he faces. One way or another, however he chooses to edit the text, he — Vincent the controller — will be complicit: Ministry-man or rebel? There is no middle ground.

He is struck by how unfair his situation has become. He always assumed the routine of going to the Ministry, doing his work, coming home, and living his quiet unassuming life would be enough for him. It is exactly the kind of life he expected to have. If he had opinions and dreams they were always small scale, modest like his existence; and he has kept them to himself, under wraps, as if they might be hidden away in a small box at the back of a drawer. But Verna's request is about to force him to open that drawer, withdraw the box, see what is inside. He closes his eyes, attempting to picture what he might find there. And once again he sees himself shopping, dismayed at the cost of boots, annoyed at the lack of choice in the clothes shop. Opening his eyes, his vision is filled with the bright red tie, as if its colour is leaking out across the surface of the table, contaminating everything it touches.

And Marina? Long since reconciled to his hopes for a wife and family remaining unfulfilled, he finds her reawakening them. That is another decision he didn't expect to face; another dilemma as to meaning; another box to be opened — or already opened. A box containing a bright red tie.

❅

Early Thursday morning finds a myriad of fingers tapping on keyboards: Verna preparing her weekly progress update; Marina drafting interim reports on the cases assigned to her; Will studiously cross-referencing notes and drawing conclusions; Marcus striving for the right kind of impartiality, alternating between email addresses — Ministry and private — the latter protected by an even more secure firewall than the one provided by his employers. At some point all four make comment on a common topic, assessments which, in one case at least, heads towards judgement and recommendation.

And what of the shared subject which unites them? Vincent's fingers spend more time hovering over keys than hitting them. On the screen in front of him, the text he needs to address. Verna has told him that she doesn't expect any kind of major overhaul; "It's more a question of tweaking for current sensibilities." Given such an instruction, Vincent had walked out of her office none the wiser; cast adrift with the only sensibilities by which he could navigate being his own. But at least he knew *something* was expected; returning the text totally unchanged would clearly be unacceptable. In any case, doing nothing would effectively be the same as doing something, inaction the equivalent to action.

As the first page dances before his eyes, Vincent wonders whether he might have become dyslexic overnight. Momentarily panicked, he stabs the cursor into the middle of the first paragraph and hits the spacebar, just to see what happens. Reassuringly a gap appears; there is an almost imperceptible shift of the characters to its right, the lines below unchanged. More importantly, they stop dancing. He hits the 'delete' key then moves his eyes up to the first word on the first page: 'If'. Although innocent enough, whole sentences cascade from that one word; not merely the sentences attempting to engage him from the screen, but new ones beginning to form in his head, a great fog of 'what ifs' that start to pose largely theoretical questions emanating from the painful hours in his kitchen the previous evening. He thinks back to the notebook and suddenly can't remember where he left it. Surely it is irrational to worry, after all no-one is going to go into his kitchen until he gets home in eight hours' time.

He goes back to the text. 'If Frank had only wanted one thing in his life, it was precisely this…' — and a disembodied voice again echoes "trust the process", so he settles his right hand on the mouse and begins to read.

Progress is slow even if, as he expected, he finds little to correct. His usual modus operandi allows him to tackle a text quickly; his eyes are trained to seek out certain trigger words and phrases, especially in over-long sentences where it is all too easy for hidden meaning to lurk. Yet in this case Vincent finds himself needing to read each paragraph slowly and more than once, searching for something else, something unwritten. What Marcus once told him chimes like a mantra in his head — "it's not what we keep out of a book that counts, but what we might put in" — and he feels like an archaeologist seeking out what has been buried, or teasing at the gaps where things once were.

He comes across a short episode where Frank and his wife are food-shopping. She is indignant at the price of things, and makes a comment to the effect that over twenty percent of their income is spent on food. Given the passage of time since the book was written, Vincent knows she would now be complaining that over twenty-five percent is lost that way — if not more. He hesitates. Is that what Verna meant when she talked about bringing the book up-to-date? He doubts it; but even as he does so, there is recognition that he *could* change it, that it would be legitimate for him to do so — and that his choice is based on something other than fact. Leave it as it is, or make it contemporaneous? It is a decision driven not by what the author intended — nor by what Marcus wanted to say (unless those were Marcus's own words!) — but by what Vincent feels must now be said. Leave it, change it, or take it out? And if left in and inflated, does it remain in plain sight or should he squirrel it away somehow, perhaps buried in a new or reconstructed longer sentence? Unable to decide, he marks the passage and resolves to come back to it when he has finished his first run-through, when he has a better understanding of the scale of the problem.

It is in this fashion that both Thursday and Friday pass. Recoiling from the prospect of coming across Marina in the canteen, Vincent spends minimal time away from his desk. In consequence, he is more tired than usual when he eventually boards a tram to take him home; a home where, for the entire weekend, the red tie occupies its place on Vincent's kitchen table like a whispering familiar. It represents another unresolved question, another choice.

At a fundamental level Vincent's decision is a simple one: is he going to wear it or not? If not, then he will either consign it to his wardrobe or dispose of it in the waste. The latter is a strangely enticing prospect. Yet he has always wanted such a tie, and it is this which forces him to leave it in plain sight, nagging, demanding he be reconciled with it. He struggles to resolve what it will mean should he choose to wear it. If he does, what will he be saying about Marina, his ambitions for a relationship with her? Vincent knows he is not self-assured enough *not* to care. At some point — inevitably — she will see him in the canteen, see her tie around his neck, and make her own assumptions. Lost in the labyrinth of question and counter-question, he wonders whether that is indeed what she wants, what *she* hopes for. Was she opening and not closing a door with her gift?

For two days he busies himself as best he can (even trying unsuccessfully to locate his notebook) until, when he goes to bed on Sunday evening — almost as tired as when he arrived home two days earlier — he has removed the tie from the table and which, as a result, will seem strangely naked when he comes down for breakfast on Monday morning.

❊

"And finally, updates on Vincent?"

Marcus looks round the table and allows his gaze to settle on Verna. It has been a difficult meeting and they are all clearly tired; the prospect of the working week ahead does nothing to help the mood.

"Well he finally got started on your book. Took him a while to do so; I think he put it off as long as he could."

"Too early to draw any conclusions?"

Verna nods. "Yes, I think so. I've been keeping an eye on the document, tracking any changes. So far, apart from minor cosmetic things, he has been bookmarking passages he clearly wants to come back to. Presumably because he hasn't yet resolved whether or not he needs to do anything with them."

"Such as?"

Verna frowns for a moment. "Oh yes, I forgot how well you know the book." She pauses. "The section where Frank and his wife are out shopping; and one in the next chapter when he's in that heated conversation at work."

"I remember it," Marcus confirms. "He hasn't reached the kitchen scene yet, the one with the letter?"

"Probably in the middle of the coming week."

"We'll see what he makes of that. It was the extract I talked through with him all those years ago. You'll keep me posted?"

Verna nods again.

"Do you think we may need to force the issue?" The question comes from Will.

"In what way?"

"Telling him we need it finished sooner. You know, the weekend-working tactic."

"I'm not sure." Marcus weighs up the option. "This is a very different case to, say, that of Noah. Don't you agree, Verna?" He doesn't wait for a response. "Far less clear cut. And with more potential outcomes."

"Well two anyway," Will offers, though not sounding as if he believes it.

"Which is more than one."

Marcus sits back in his chair and runs his hand through his hair, glancing at Marina as he does so. Everyone can see how tired he is.

"Marina has been doing some digging," he volunteers, "just as you would expect her too. Trying to apply a little pressure from an alternative perspective."

"And?" Will again.

"Inconclusive, wouldn't you say?"

Now it is Marina's turn to nod. "There's one prompt from which we're awaiting a response."

"And," Marcus interjects before she can elaborate, "we have come across something else — evidence of a sort — that we need to consider. But we've only had it a couple of days, so it's also too early to draw conclusions from that. I'll let you see it once I've digested it."

"And by the middle of the week?" Will asks.

"I suppose we might have a few more clues, a few more answers."

"And a decision?"

"Perhaps next Sunday, who knows? And don't forget, we may choose to do nothing at all." Another glance to Marina. "Let's see how things play out. My honest opinion is that at this stage it's too close to call, so I'm glad I'm not a betting man."

It is an assertion which fails to ring true with the others, especially Marina. More than anyone, she is acutely aware of the trajectory of her father's life over the previous few years, the decisions he made, the risks he ran. Indeed, the risks he is still running. As they all are.

❊

People are looking. As he waits at the tram-stop he feels their eyes linger on him a little longer than usual. They are not exactly staring but rather indulging in a second-take of sorts, as if they cannot help but check what they have seen. A bell's ring forces them to glance in the direction of the approaching tram. Bags are retrieved from where they had been resting on the pavement and are re-shouldered; knowing it will be warm in the upcoming press of bodies, a number of coat buttons are undone. Vincent places a hand in his jacket pocket to check once more that he has his usual blue tie — in case he loses his nerve.

The tram proves to be less of a trial than he had expected. Theirs is a throng of contact avoidance, and Vincent scans other faces to see how many of his fellow commuters are drawn to the startling flash of red. Catching the eye of one or two (who then immediately look away), he wonders what they might be thinking, the questions they could be asking themselves. Expecting to be discomforted by this modest level of attention, he finds himself bizarrely warmed by it. Whether it is some obscure elevation of status, or in those brief eye-to-eye connections, but the tie *has* made a difference; he feels as if it has shifted his place in the world ever so slightly.

And what of Marina? This is what he is thinking as he walks across the Market Square towards the Ministry. How will she react to his wearing her tie? He speculated on that most of Sunday evening, grist to his decision-making mill. More significantly perhaps, he tried to decode what *he* hoped the outcome would be. He has concocted scenes in his head where she sees him — or rather, the tie — across the canteen and walks straight over, takes his hand, kisses him on the cheek. These were scenes where something was settled. No words were needed. There were other scenarios of course, with less positive outcomes; but it had been the happier to which he returned most often. Presumably, he concluded, that in itself meant something too.

As he walks through the office, those who are already there look up, offer their usual greeting. Trying to make out that nothing is different, Vincent does likewise — all the while unable not to note those who are drawn to the area just beneath his chin. There are a small number of comments. "Nice tie" is offered more than once. One person ventures "Vincent's got himself a girl!" in a voice loud enough to ensure the comment is heard by those nearby. Walking out of earshot, Vincent misses the response — "so he's not a virgin any more" — but hears the laughter which follows it.

The approach to his desk is coincident with Verna making her way back to her office from the kitchen area, coffee cup in hand. She looks at the tie, then to his face. "Morning Vincent," she says, "busy week ahead." It is one of her standard lines. Less standard is her entering her office and immediately closing the door behind her. As Vincent removes his coat he watches Verna as she puts down the mug and addresses her computer. Beyond the glass walls of her office, Verna opens a new email and begins typing.

❖

As if I didn't have enough to worry about, now there's this. The tie to go along with the book. What am I supposed to do now? Having one problem should be enough for anyone. But two? It almost feels as if people are ganging up on me. And Life too. "Vincent", it's saying, "you've had it easy for far too long, the same old routine, sticking to convention. Time to find out what you're made of." Some joke. I don't think I've deserved this — though having said that, I'm not really sure what 'this' is...

And if I asked myself which of the two is the bigger problem, the harder conundrum to solve?

Sitting here, with the tie right in front of me, in my eye-line, making the colours of everything else in the kitchen seem pale by comparison... It's kind of insistent. Demanding. As if it's challenging me to answer the question as to where it belongs. Bright Life versus Dull Life.

But that's also a question of where ███ belongs. In or out? Part of my life or not? Problem or solution? And how the hell am I supposed to resolve that when I don't know what it is <u>she</u> wants, what the tie is supposed to mean — because it must mean something. No-one sends a present just for the hell of it, do they? ~~All of which makes my decision somehow secondary, almost irrelevant.~~

What if I decide I want her to be in my life and she doesn't? If she just laughs in my face, slams the door shut again? "I don't think so, do you?" The tie more a 'goodbye' than a 'hello'…

Who'd have thought a scrap of cloth could be so problematic?

I should get changed, make supper… But not just yet. Because of the other question. The book.

What's to stop me just doing my job, treating Frank's story as if I'd never seen it before, as if Verna had simply dumped it on my desk, the next anonymous novel to work on in a long line of novels?

Because it isn't. Because I have seen it before. Because of Marcus. Because I know more about it than I should — and maybe less about it than I want to…

Choices. I didn't ask for choices, but they have been forced upon me.

…

Okay, just think about it for a minute.

How well do I know Frank's story? Or rather, Marcus's version of it? ~~Well enough to decipher the hidden messages, the underlying code? Let's face it, it's the philosophy that got him killed.~~

Yes, there's the kitchen scene he pointed out to me, the odd word here and there, especially in what Frank's wife says; words —

individual little words — which do so much heavy lifting. Words that say one thing and yet... Can I find the others, however many of them there may be? Probably not all, but surely some of them. I have to back myself to find them, partly because of my experience — and because I <u>know</u> they're there. And because I want to find them? That gets to the heart of it perhaps.

Like clues, I have an inkling of what I'm looking for; I can ask the questions "why this word, and not that word?", "why describe it in this way when it would be more conventional to do so in that way?". Some words will leap off the page, even if they wouldn't for most people...

So if I give myself credit for being able to do that, for successful excavation, what next?

What to do with them, that's the rub. Replace the unconventional with the conventional? Diffuse the incendiary? Neuter the text, make it bland, homogenous? Turn it from the exceptional and unique to the banal?

Do my job?

That would be the safe approach. I'd hand back to Verna a text that was antiseptic, inoffensive, unremarkable, safe. Safe. Safe. I could aim to just get it out of the way, keep my head down, be the good citizen. Is that what Verna's expecting? Does she even know what she's given me? How can she?

Surely that's the way forward; keep it simple, risk-free. That and throwing the tie away...

But I don't know. I'm not sure. I wonder if that approach — the easy and 'safe' approach — is somehow dishonest. I wonder whether it would be traitorous to <u>myself</u>.

[...I've just re-read the above, and I think the key is in that last paragraph. I can't get away from the feeling that I need to be authentic, honest...]

Do I even know what that looks like any more?

Do I?

And am I the same me from three weeks ago? Or last year? Or before I met Marcus?

If there were no potential repercussions, if I could have the outcome I really wanted — what would that look like?

Stand in-front of the mirror of yourself Vincent; what do you see?

Not a conventional revolutionary, that's for sure! ~~But p~~ *Perhaps a man who believes in something after all. The power of books.* ~~And a woman.~~ *Perhaps I didn't know that until now. Or recently. Or maybe I've always known it; a trigger was needed, that's all. Or triggers. A book and a tie.*

What does the Vincent reflected back to me believe?

That he should be able to buy a tie of any colour he chooses? Probably, yes. That people should be free to express themselves, write what they want to? ~~Ditto.~~ *That people like him shouldn't be needed to validate and sanitise texts? That things should be cheaper; that the old parts of town should be revitalised; that more people should enjoy and embrace their lives?* ~~Yes, of course.~~

That anyone should be able to read Frank's story, unexpurgated?

That Marcus shouldn't have been killed for believing those same things?

Answer the questions, Vincent. Answer the questions.

And ▮▮▮▮▮▮*? Is her part of the equation less within my control? Are any of the potential outcomes* ~~as far as she is concerned~~

within my compass? If I close my eyes and think of ███, *what do I see? How do I see her? Where is she? Where are <u>we</u>?*

I look at the tie again, as if it might possess answers to all the questions. As if there might be some intrinsic link, the tie being the thing that — well — ties it all together: the book, Frank's story, ███ *Marcus, everything.*

~~*And my future too.*~~

Satisfied, Marcus clicks 'save' and prepares to send the slightly amended copy to Will ("the woman's name is unimportant right now"); then he opens the filing cabinet sitting alongside his desk, and places Vincent's blue notebook inside.

❋

On the third floor of the Ministry building there are fewer offices. Those that are there, tucked just under the fabric of the roof, are larger than elsewhere; some — with oak, teak or mahogany desks — betray an opulence which the rooms' occupants argue is only allowed to exist in order to serve as a reminder of the past. A self-indulgent past. In some rooms, desks are supplemented by a small round meeting table, and others — the largest and most luxurious — boast at least two armchairs and perhaps a bookcase or drinks cabinet. Few people have ever seen inside such offices. For most Ministry workers they are the stuff of rumour and legend.

Behind an unlabelled door in a room not far from the single lift which permits access to this floor, three men sit at such a meeting table. A cup and saucer (all empty now) rests in front of each of them. Two of the men —

one tall and lean, the other shorter, bespectacled — have portfolios in front of them. Both files are shut.

"We are close then?" The man wearing glasses asks the third. The tallest man momentarily opens his folder, glances at the uppermost sheet of paper, and then closes it again.

"Very, I would say."

"And you are certain of that outcome?"

"I think so."

"In all three cases?" The tall man asks, seeking clarity.

"I'm sure I can force the issue in the case of the least significant one."

"'Least significant'?"

"The catalyst. A nobody."

"And the other two? The main prize — if you're right that is?" Turning his head towards the tall man, the light from the desk lamp reflects from his glasses for a moment. "We have to be sure," he says earnestly, "people up here are uncomfortable." The tall man nods.

"I'm convinced. Completely." Their guest again.

"And the evidence?"

"Will be indisputable; what happens to the catalyst, how the others respond, will be all the proof I need. Then I'll send you both the full tile. We'll be able to act inside two weeks."

Both senior men reopen their portfolios in concert, as if it is a rehearsed move. The third man waits for a moment.

"I doubt we will need to do anything excessive or punitive in the third case."

"A minor player?" suggests the man with glasses.

"Indeed. A pawn really." A pause. "But…"

About to close their folders, the two older men look the way of their guest.

"But?" echoes the tall man, beating the other to the punch.

"There may be a fourth person."

Checking his folder again, the bespectacled man looks up. "There's nothing here to suggest a fourth."

"I know. A recent development. There is an attachment of sorts — but that attachment may be of a more significant nature than I had at first imagined."

"Any danger?" The tall man.

"For us?"

Both senior men nod.

"I don't think so. Indeed, it may offer you an even greater coup."

Smiling, the shorter man stands; offers his hand across the table.

"And you too. You too."

✽

"He was wearing the tie today."

"Yes, I know."

"How so? Did you get an email from Verna too?"

Marina looks at her father across the lounge. From the kitchen, sounds of her mother making supper.

"I saw him. In the canteen. I walked in and there he was, paying at the checkout." She laughs a little. "It shone like a beacon!"

"I'm not surprised; I've always liked that tie." Marcus takes a sip of his drink, a sherry before dinner. "Still, it must have taken something for him to wear it."

"What do you mean?"

"Guts, I suppose." He considers the notion. "After all, he's not the most flamboyant of people, is he? Reserved, cautious. If you think about it from that perspective…"

Marina is about to accept the space seemingly offered her but it disappears when her father continues speaking.

"Did you talk to him?"

"No. I just turned around and left. Didn't go back to the canteen for the rest of the day, and then came home early just to ensure I didn't bump into him."

"Because?"

It is the only logical question, and one she knew would arise at some point. Even so, Marina finds she has no suitable answer for him; none she can adequately articulate nor that she wishes to share.

"I don't know." She waits a moment to see if he picks up on her uncertainty. He doesn't. "I didn't want a scene, I suppose. Over the weekend I thought about what I'd do if I saw him with it on; I tried to decide why he might choose to wear it given I treated him so badly…"

"Any conclusions?"

Marina knows her father has already completed his own deductions, so this is represents a test. As an only child, he was always challenging her: her reading; her athleticism; her cooking.

"To send a message. Either he wanted me to see that he hasn't given up on me — in spite of where we left off the other day — or it was a statement of defiance."

"Defiance?"

"Yes. Maybe he has arrived at the least charitable conclusion possible, and wanted me to see that he was stronger than I'd supposed, not someone who was going to crumble; that maybe he didn't need me as much as I thought he might."

"An act of rebellion?"

Marcus's mischievous smile makes Marina laugh. "If you want to portray it that way... But you know how these things are: by Thursday the tie will have ceased to have any meaning; no-one will notice he's wearing it any more, not even him."

A call from the kitchen triggers them both to stand.

"And what about you?" Marcus asks.

"Me?"

"You don't feel compromised in any way?"

"Only in that there may be an awkward coming together at some point."

"That's not what I meant."

"I know it isn't."

＊

Vincent is clearing away the dishes from his Wednesday evening meal when there is a knock at his front door. Not expecting anyone, he finishes drying the plate in his hands and then deposits both it and the tea-towel onto the work surface. The intervening few seconds are long enough for there to be a second knock.

Opening the door he finds himself facing a woman in a heavy coat, her face shaded by its hood pulled over her head and from beneath which a mass of hair falls onto her shoulders. It is only when she speaks that he recognises her.

"Can I come in?"

"Marina."

Once in the hallway, she slips the coat from her shoulders and almost absentmindedly hands it to him. He hangs it on a peg and follows her into the lounge. She has paused by the sofa, then turns to face him as he enters the room.

"You wore the tie," she says, part statement, part question.

"I didn't recognise you — the dark, and all that hair." It is a similar opening, with the exception that his words are laced with confusion.

"This?" She awards his statement priority and briefly runs the fingers of her left hand through her hair. "A wig, obviously."

"Obviously."

There is a different tone in his voice, not one which had been present the last time Marina was in the room. Perhaps she shouldn't be surprised.

"I used to have long hair when I was a child. Well, until a few years ago, actually. And then things happened. Mainly the job at the Ministry I suppose. Long hair didn't seem to fit."

"Fit?"

"You wore the tie," she says again, returning to her original theme.

Now it is his turn to yield. "I did, yes. You saw it then?"

"On Monday." She pauses, unsure how quickly to nudge the conversation forward. "I was half-expecting you to throw it in the bin given how badly I had behaved."

"Probably not the bin," Vincent says, softening slightly. "Banishing it to the back of a drawer perhaps."

"A keepsake for the future?" she suggests; then a little more mischievously, "Or a trophy?"

"Hardly that." It is a notion that has never occurred to him; how could it? "But it wasn't an easy decision. All things considered." He thinks about confessing to having had a blue tie in his pocket all that morning, then decides against it. "But I did."

"And?"

"'And'?"

She smiles a little, then sits down. Vincent edges closer, but remains standing.

"Doing so was — I don't know — a little radical, don't you think? A bright red tie in a sea of blue ones."

Vincent laughs, then tangentially remembers the pots and cutlery sitting in the kitchen awaiting salvation. "It certainly got me noticed. And drew a few comments from my co-workers. That didn't last long really; this morning there was nothing. But all that wasn't important anyway."

"Oh? What was?"

"The fact that I'd always wanted a tie like that. And now I have one; so why not wear it?"

"Even though it had been given to you by an evil and callous woman?"

"I don't think you're evil."

"Well then." Even if his statement is merely rewarding her with second prize, it is enough to make her stand. "No other reason? I was hoping it might have meant that I was forgiven for a second time."

Frozen, Vincent hears her request for further absolution, then watches as her hands — seemingly in slow motion — once again reach for the buttons on his shirt.

❊

Apologies for the late email, V, but I think we need to accelerate the process in respect of Vincent. I want matters brought to a head quickly. And for a number of reasons. I don't think we can wait for him to jump one way or the other on his own accord.

Can we apply some pressure? I was thinking of using the shorter deadline excuse and getting him to work through the weekend. I know the circumstances are very different to those with Noah -

not least in that the outcome here is in the balance - but I need this resolved. We need to know on whose side Vincent is going to settle.

I have an idea, but I want proof.

Unless I hear otherwise, I'll assume you're okay with this as a plan. I'll let Will know.

Perhaps we should arrange to meet in the usual place on Sunday, around five? And if you can bring Vincent, obviously…

M.

*

"What is this?" Vincent asks, more to the ceiling than the woman resting in the crook of his arm.

"What do you think it is?" Her hand still resting on his thigh, Marina gives his flesh a soft pinch. "What do you mean anyway?"

He allows his fingers to stroke her waist just above the left hip. "The last two weeks have been pretty surreal," and then, almost as an afterthought, "pretty much since I met you."

"Me?"

"Not that you've anything to do with my work of course, so that's merely coincidence." He kisses her lightly on the top of her head.

"What is?"

"Things getting weird at work."

She shuffles her position slightly, doing so causes her hand to gently brush his penis.

"They've asked me to re-edit a book for a re-issue."

"Is there anything unusual in that?"

"Not particularly — though re-issues are relatively rare."

"So?"

"The book. Its previous editor was Marcus F.; you know, that guy who was…"

"Executed." She interrupts, keen to prove both her knowledge and that she is listening.

Vincent allows a small break to work its way into the conversation. His fingers continue their rhythmical circle-making on Marina's skin. "Did I tell you I once met him?"

"Marcus?"

"He came to a careers event at college; talked to us about what a controller did."

"Surely there's nothing remarkable about that?"

"And then I met him afterwards. Later." He continues as if she hadn't spoken at all. "You know, just me and him. I had questions; I was interested. And he showed me this book he'd edited. He was trying to illustrate something about the work he did, the skill involved."

"And let me guess: that's the book you've been asked to edit?"

"Yes."

Letting out a soft dismissive laugh, Marina's fingers now move very softly where they rest. "But that's just another coincidence, surely."

"Perhaps. But this book. Marcus talked to me about how it was possible — I don't know — to include other messages in the text. Given what he did, what happened to him, he could only have meant subversive ones couldn't he? He talked about what to leave in, or not take out; that editing could be about adding too."

"And that's what makes you nervous about tacking this book?"

"The basic process, no." He glances down to the top of her head, then to where she is stretched out beneath the sheet. "But trying to find those things he left in, or put in. To uncover them, if you like — because they're not easy to find, a word here a word there."

"So you can put it right?"

"'Right'? I'm not sure I know what that means any more." Another pause. "The question is, when I find something — if I find something — that has Marcus's fingerprints all over it, what do I do? Can I be sure that it's him and not the original author? And if they're 'incendiary', can I be certain I've interpreted the words correctly? Do I take them out, or leave them in? As the new controller, what's left in the final version of the book is my edit, not Marcus's; it will be based on what I think and believe, not on what he thought back then. Do you see?"

Whether Marina can understand or not, she doesn't say. Beneath her fingers she can feel Vincent stirring again. It is enough to deflect him.

"What's going on?" he asks playfully. "I need some sleep before I go to work in the morning."

"So do I," she says, then twists her body so that she is laying full-length along his. He is trapped and powerless. "And it's tomorrow already."

*

"You can handle this?"

Marcus had hesitated when making the call. He distrusted telephones; there was no body language to read and you could never be sure who was listening.

"Of course," says Will from somewhere else, "after all, I had the best teacher. And I don't mean the late and unlamented Simpson." He laughs.

"He was a tricky bastard," Marcus chooses not to acknowledge the compliment, "I never liked him, especially after our first encounter."

"Which was, for me, quite memorable of course — though I had no idea that one day I'd be working for the guy who was being interrogated."

"Working with, not for." It is one of Marcus's favourite lines, though he is unsure if he believes it in the same way he once did. He changes tack slightly. "Verna's confirmed that she'll be there with Vincent at five."

"You'll be there?"

"Close enough; able to see and hear everything."

"And Marina?"

"I'm not sure." Marcus knows he has to be careful. "I think she's been involved enough to this point; it may not be appropriate for her to go through the whole denouement."

Will lets it go. "Which will be?"

Although he knows that from Will's perspective the verdict is centred on a binary choice — and given Will has been unimpressed with Vincent, the odds are stacked in favour of a negative outcome — Marcus isn't convinced they have reached that stage. Things are much less cut-and-dried than Will can possible know. Unless Vincent does something radical over the next three days — all the way up to the Sunday deadline — it is entirely possible that the situation will remain fluid a while longer, his future in limbo. In a way, Marina's too. And how would Marcus define radical? Vincent either handing the book in with Marcus's own heavily disguised messages still within it (or even enhanced!), or significantly edited and sanitised. The latter offers the simplest outcome.

"Driven by the text," Marcus eventually replies, "and what he does with it. Or does not do. Verna is keeping track of progress; she has access to all the versions he's creating, all the edits he makes. She'll email her summary around four-thirty. We'll see if it's cut-and-dried then."

"And if it is?"

"Then your session with him will progress pretty much as mine did with Simpson. He'll either be with us or against us."

There is silence for a moment. Marcus is about to speak again when Will responds.

"And making that decision?"

"You leave the room for a moment to come and find me so that we can concur, or I come in."

"But he'll recognise you."

It is a circumstance Marcus has already considered. "You're right, of course. I doubt the beard, the subtle hair dye, the glasses, and being — what? — nine years older will be sufficient disguise. All of which means that, if I do come in, we'll have to be certain. *I'll* have to be certain. Under those circumstances — me walking into the room — the 'wait and see' option goes out of the window."

Marcus senses another question coming, so waits.

"And Verna will be there throughout?"

"Sitting in the corner, acting as witness."

"Or safety valve?" Will suggests.

Marcus laughs. "You're not that kind of character, Will." And in this final silence, the ghost of Simpson still with them, Marcus wonders how true his statement is.

❋

It is mid-way through Thursday when Marina opens the email.

I'm going to have to take a rain-check on our trip to the country. They've brought forward the deadline for this damned book and I have to try and get it done by the end of Sunday afternoon — which means working all weekend. It's going better now I've decided what I'm doing, so I might just finish it in time.

I know you were looking forward to the trip. Sorry. Maybe the following weekend?

Vincent x

And of course Marina is disappointed. The jaunt had been Vincent's idea, and she'd been only too pleased to go along with it. Yet while she is disappointed, she is not surprised. Indeed, she already knew what was being arranged for the weekend. Now the only question is whether or not her burgeoning disquiet is going to prompt her into action.

＊

Finally resolved on what he believes is right, Vincent accelerates through his work on Friday. Having settled on the approach — knowing, for example, what he is going to do with Frank's kitchen scene — he abandons himself to his process. He has come to understand that all he needed to do was to come to terms with the editing challenge not as a textual one, but rather driven by the philosophical and political. Finishing by Sunday's deadline suddenly seems achievable.

He wants to give credit to Marina, not that she has helped him in any practical sense. As far as he is aware she has not read the book in question, nor have they discussed the task he faces in any detail. What she has done is overlay the human on the everyday, give him a perspective he was lacking. Process and text is all very well, but it can be as cold and uninspiring as a number 10 tram-ride in the depths of winter. Marina has reaffirmed the importance of affection, human contact, trust. And even if it is no more than a reawakening, Vincent cannot recall when he felt the way he does now.

The suggestion of the weekend away was made because he suddenly realised that it was something he could do. It is not as fashionable a prospect as it once had been — largely because there are few suitable destinations remaining — but it *is* still possible. Such a trip would be a way to make a statement not only about his affection for her, but about his life too, that he still has choices. Sitting at his desk late on Friday afternoon — his email to her long since sent — he again catches a glimpse of his tie. It is another example of what is possible. Not only a statement from Marina as to what she thinks of him, it has also come to represent assertion of freedom. He *can* own such a tie, wear such a thing to work. It is out of the ordinary certainly, but it is also about something far more important.

In their initial training controllers are encouraged to "leave your self at the front door"; "books are not about you", they are told, "your sole interest is in accuracy, repairing typographical errors, resolving clumsy writing, being true to the philosophy of our culture." It is a mantra metaphorically beaten in to them during their probation period. Vincent has seen people fail the training because they have been unable to manifest such a separation. And he has seen others — Noah being the most recent example — where the self crashes back into the process, takes over, undoes all the training. It is because of this that, even in his present euphoria, Vincent fears where his new attachment to 'freedom' may lead. He has mapped out a simple enough path: he will hand in the book, move on to something else, go away with Marina the following weekend. He tells himself it will be the same life as before but embellished, given colour; yet he also knows abandoning the monochrome is about more than a trip to the countryside or wearing a red tie to work.

✻

Both,

Vincent is now making great progress. He seems to have found his stride and is confident of finishing by five on Sunday. Most of his edits are typographical or structural — the usual sort of thing — but some require eyes other than my own to decipher and deconstruct them. I will send you some examples via courier.

V.

✻

"I may go away for a couple of days, if that's okay."

Marcus looks up from the table where he is finishing the remnants of his Saturday-morning breakfast, his hand just about to turn a page in a report he has been reading. Standing by the kitchen door on the way back to her room, Marina has delivered her words in as off-hand a manner as she could muster.

"Oh? Do you think you need my permission?"

"Not really. I only mentioned it in case you needed me for anything today. Or tomorrow."

"Nothing I can think of." He completes the turning of the page in front of him. "Where will you go?"

"I've an old friend from college who's temporarily moved to a place up near the lakes. She's working on her thesis for a second degree and I think she's a bit lonely; I said

I'd go and keep her company for an evening or two, go for a walk tomorrow. That's all."

"Sounds like a good plan. Have you told your mother?"

Marina nods. "I mentioned it to her late yesterday. She was fine with it, but I just wanted to check with you. I'll take the small jeep, if that's ok — in case the road's difficult."

He looks toward the window as if verifying something. "Which it may well be this time of year, once you're off the main roads." Marina makes to go. "You'll send us a message to let us know you've got there alright? And tell us when you're on your way back?"

Marina steps back to the table and kisses her father on the top of his head. "Of course."

Not that she is going to the forest. There is no friend there to see. Imaginary friend notwithstanding, she will leave the house and go somewhere, perhaps just a little way out of town, stay overnight in an anonymous motorway motel — even if they are a little run-down these days. Pay in cash; use a false name. Later, she'll let her father know she has ostensibly arrived; and in the morning find somewhere to walk, just to get her thoughts together.

Rarely confused, there is something about the business with Vincent which has thrown her off balance. Against her better judgement she has allowed her involvement to trespass beyond the professional contribution requested by her father. In that context, sending the tie was meant to bookend her involvement; yet seeing him wearing it had unexpectedly opened a door of sorts, and — though the stakes had become higher than she could ever have envisaged — she has chosen to walk straight through it.

*

As he had been three Fridays previously, Vincent is struck by the different demographic of Saturday morning tram passengers. Treating it like a weekday, he has woken at the usual time and dressed in the normal way for a day in the office. Although he knows he shouldn't be surprised to be the only man on the tram in a suit and tie, he is still vaguely unsettled. Shop-workers heading into town are wearing their own uniforms of course: someone from the shoe shop through whose window he so recently browsed; two women from the mini-supermarket on the square; and two older men in the green fatigues of the Botanical Gardens. Behind him, talking in whispers, a young couple stand either side of a suitcase. He assumes they are making their way to the railway station, and can't help but wonder where they are going and how long they will be away. Their presence makes him think of Marina. The tram fills gradually as it gets closer to the centre of town, the two Botanical Gardens' workers the only people to disembark. And when it arrives in the Market Square almost everyone gets off, all except the suitcase couple, two more stops to the station.

Arriving at his department, he is surprised to see the light on in Verna's office, the door open, his boss sitting behind her desk. He suspects Fran may be around too. Verna looks up at his approach.

"I didn't expect to see you here," he says, lightly. "Do you also have a deadline?"

She laughs half-heartedly. "Of sorts. I have to run some errands in town this morning, so thought I'd just pop-in to close off a few things that eluded me at the end of yesterday."

Vincent then notices that she is casually dressed — though in Verna's case that still means there is a certain smartness about her; even when off-duty she has the air of a professional woman. As he turns to his desk, he realises how little he knows about her. Is she married? Does she have children?

"You made good progress at the end of last week," she says, stopping him. It is part statement, part not. "Optimistic of hitting the deadline?"

"Reasonably. Most of the mundane edits are done — tidying up the odd sentence here and there, replacing outmoded words." He pauses to consider his use of 'outmoded', knowing there are other ways to express what he means. "There are a few more troublesome passages, though. I'll get to those later today, early tomorrow. Then I should be done. At the moment I'm reasonably confident that I'll get the final version to you before five."

"That's splendid. Thank you. And then, of course, you'll have to let me know when you'd like to take the time-off in lieu — or whether you want paying for it instead."

"One day paid, one day off." If Verna's question is delivered somewhat haltingly, his reply is immediate, "with Monday week being the day off. If that's ok?" If he and Marina are to have a weekend away together, they should make the most of it.

Verna nods. "I'm sure that will be fine — but let's get through tomorrow first."

*

"What's the latest?" Will looks across the small round table in room 1.49; Marcus is sitting opposite him. On the table is a laptop computer; on its screen, the table and chairs of the currently unoccupied room two doors away.

"Finished, and heading this way in about ten minutes."

"Does he know why he's coming here?"

Marcus notes something slightly odd in the younger man's tone. Perhaps it is a reflection of nervousness.

"Final validation. I think that was how Verna described it to him; a little like a viva after an exam. Vincent knows there are checking processes; he has seen the output from their findings — though the controller themselves is rarely present at such events. Hopefully, on that basis, he won't be too surprised."

"Or suspicious."

"Indeed." Marcus watches Will stand. "You've read the excerpts Verna sent through — including the latest one about an hour ago."

"I have."

"And?"

Will rests a hand on the back of the chair he has just vacated; leans against it.

"He's clearly made changes."

"Clearly. His experience is showing through. I was impressed."

"'Impressed'?"

"By how subtle some of the changes were." Marcus finds himself wondering whether Vincent's ingenuity might have been missed by his colleague. "Subtle not only in that most often it's just the odd word here and there, but also because of what those words do to the underlying meaning and message. Adjectives can be very powerful; or the choice of a marginally less concrete verb. Easy to miss."

If the last phrase is offered as a way of forgiving Will his lack of hands-on experience as a controller, he ignores it.

"But still relatively cut-and-dried."

"You think so?"

Unsure whether or not Marcus is testing him, Will decides to be decisive. "Unquestionably." It is, he knows, a gambit not without risk; after all, are not each and every one of them always under supervision, one way or another? Assessment and judgement, the name of the game — and he has made his own choices, drawn his own conclusions. "There are passages still extant that you might argue we could have expected to see altered or removed."

"Depending on the position he was taking," Marcus prompts, unsure of Will's reasoning.

"Indeed. And where they haven't been… And the few changed words, the inferences, the clarifications. Isn't it clear which side he favours?"

Even after all this time Marcus is uncomfortable with the notion of 'sides'. He has been playing the game too long. Indeed, he has been on both sides, in appearance or in reality; danced along that tightrope knowing there was nothing but a hard fall on either side. It is still that way. Wisdom tells him that all he can openly do is concur, though for the moment he is unsure exactly what he is agreeing with. "On the balance of probability, yes."

He wonders how much his own assessment has been influenced by Marina's involvement — or by his own. And how much that might affect the outcome too. The book was his before it was Vincent's; the words that have or have not been manipulated were — at some practical level — his own; the messages conveyed (or denied) his too. In re-reading segments of the text — a text now a complex blend of the original overlaid with both his and Vincent's modifications — Marcus tries to recall what he believed back then. Indeed, what he believes now. Obtusely, he wonders if he is just getting old.

Irrespective of 'side', once he had been like Will: young, idealistic, thrusting, keen to get on. Marcus thinks back to when he was face-to-face with Simpson, Will sitting in the corner of the room. You always knew where you were with Simpson; but Marcus finds himself suddenly unsure if he can be so certain about Will. People seem much more complex these days. Indeed, who can ever really know what another person believes.

"You have a verdict in mind?" Then before Will can respond, Marcus chases the phrase away. "Not a verdict, that's the wrong choice of word. You have settled on Vincent's underlying position; you have a view on what he has been trying to do with this book?" He returns to the tightrope. "The side on which he has fallen?"

Will ignores the potential for ambiguity, uncertainty, for doing nothing, and — bypassing words — simply nods.

Marcus wonders if it is profoundly ridiculous that the two of them should be the arbiters of Vincent's motives, second-guessing what he was trying to do. And Marina? What is Vincent's intention in her case — assuming he has one? The last email from Verna (to him alone) mentioned the desire for a long weekend, and Marcus can do nothing but see in that an echo of Marina's choosing to go away this one. Everything is connected; he has always believed that. In this instance Marcus wants the naïve to be triumphant, yet whichever way the next hour or so goes, he fears the repercussions.

"And therefore you have a recommendation in mind?" Marcus asks.

"I do — unless he manages to say something which changes what I think. One way or the other."

If it strikes Marcus as an odd but highly pertinent phrase, he lets it go.

"So you will interview him, see where that gets you, then come here and see me. Bring Verna if you need to — but I'd rather you didn't. Then we'll concur. Agreed?"

"Of course."

Will straightens, then leaves the room. Ten seconds later Marcus watches as he enters room 1.51, glances up to the hidden camera in acknowledgement, then sits down with his back to it.

They both wait.

❋

It being Sunday afternoon the roads are reasonably clear. There was a time when this had not been the case, when more people would go away for the weekend and Sundays witness the inevitable influx back into the city. If Marina has recollections of such days, she knows such memories are manufactured; she would have been sitting in the back of her father's car, returning from a visit to her grandparents or her aunt and uncle on her mother's side. Back then, such journeys passed in something of a dull blur, excused the requirement to concentrate as she does now. Allowing her eyes to momentarily skip down to the dashboard, she registers the time. It is already nearly five. She is conscious that she may have made her decision too late.

They will meet in room 1.51. They always meet in room 1.51. And she has more than a vague idea as to what may transpire. Her father's personal testimony is the most authentic history available, both of when he was under suspicion himself and later when sitting in judgement on others. Since his confrontation with Simpson — which she knows he has always sugar-coated for her consumption — he has taken that same role himself: asked the questions, made assessments. Perhaps even tied the knots. If he has sugar-coated those experiences too, she has, until this moment, always been grateful. But now the man she so recently slept with is the one sitting across the table, the one being judged. Marina wishes she was closer to the raw facts of the matter. Throughout the drive she has explored the spectrum between polite conversation and violent torture, visiting all points in between. She fears for Vincent at both extremes, concerned that the former might lure him into a lack of caution. And the latter? Surely he would crumble at the first instance of pain. Or even the hint of pain. And though she has no desire to believe inflicting such agony would sit well with her father — indeed, that it is not part of his make-up — he *has* sat in that room more than once and done *something*.

And this time Will is intimately involved.

She has never trusted Will. He has always seemed too keen, too sharp for her; his ambition is both obvious and inscrutably cloaked. And she is certain that he has always wanted her — which can only exacerbate the danger Vincent is in. Beneath his polite but slippery surface, Marina is convinced he is disguising something else, something steely, harder; there is a ruthlessness buried there. When Marcus has occasionally spoken of Simpson, Marina has imposed those weasel-like attributes onto an image of Will and found the fit all too glove-like. It is enough, this inheritance, for her to tell herself that she is racing back to protect Vincent not from her father, not from the process, but from Will. Amongst the narratives available to her — *all* the narratives available to her — that one is perhaps the most credible.

❊

"Thank you for that summary, Vincent." Will pauses, glances to the volume that sits on the table between them. "I have a couple of questions about what you have done with this book, but first I'd like to ask you about your character."

Even though the other man is being entirely affable, Vincent is thrown.

"My character?"

"A few observations, that's all. Just to get your reaction."

In room 1.49 Marcus leans back in his chair. Standard procedure; he and Will have discussed and rehearsed this. Meanwhile, on a road into the city, a small Jeep is delayed at a set of roadworks.

"You know Fran B., of course." Will glances to where Verna sits in the corner, then back to Vincent.

"Yes, of course." He is thrown by the question.

"Do you like her?"

It strikes Vincent as an odd thing to ask. "I can't say I've ever thought about Fran in that way. She's very efficient. I can't say I dislike her."

"Do you know what she thinks of you?"

Vincent shakes his head.

Will pulls a sheet of paper from an inner jacket pocket. Unfolds it.

"She says — and I quote — 'Vincent can be a little officious and cold. There's something about him I don't quite trust'." Will lets her words hang in the air for a moment. "Does that surprise you?"

"Yes, it does."

"Which part?"

"Both I suppose." Vincent considers the two observations. "The second part more so."

"That she doesn't trust you?"

Vincent nods.

"What is there not to trust, I wonder?" Will makes a show of consulting the sheet of paper again. "And" — he feigns hesitation — "Mrs Carsington?"

"Mrs Carsington, yes. My neighbour. What about her?"

"It seems she's not entirely enamoured with you either."

"I don't see…"

Two doors down, Marcus leans forward again. Elsewhere a red traffic-light flips to green.

"She thinks you are a man of loose morals. She has seen various women arriving at your house in the last few days." Will consults the paper. "'Various'; that's her word. Is that true Vincent?"

"It is not." Vincent is relieved he can tell the truth with confidence. "One woman; only one."

"Yet Mrs Carsington is quite certain. Two young women, looking very different. At least two."

Marina's wig. "Then she is mistaken."

"Who were these women?" Will's tone is slippery. He is making it clear that there is something other than a case of mistaken identity in play here.

"I'd rather not say. And as I said, it's only one woman. In any case, isn't my personal life my own business?"

"Is it? Do you really think that?" Any trace of benevolence in Will's voice disappears. "Your own business, Vincent? And do you therefore draw a line between yourself and the State, a line the latter party should not cross?"

"I've never thought of it in that way."

"And doing so, are you happy where that line is drawn, or do you think it should be shifted somehow? Are you resentful, perhaps? Disgruntled? Do you object to what I suppose you'd call 'influence' or 'intrusion'?"

"If you mean that nosey busy-body I live next door to…"

"You have demonstrated as much."

Will's bald statement following on from a barrage of rhetorical questions throws Vincent.

"Demonstrated what?"

"I have a statement here" — the paper again — "from an assistant who works in a gentlemen's outfitters not far from this very building." Will looks up, offers a pause. "He states that you went into his shop looking for a new tie, and when you could not find one you liked you became 'agitated'. He says that you tried to knock over a rail of garments."

Vincent laughs. If it is an unconvincing laugh it is only because he feels the interview is descending into farce.

"I bumped into one on the way out."

"Really?"

"It was an accident."

Will slips the piece of paper back into his jacket, then allows the same hand to rest momentarily on another pocket before standing and leaning on the table.

"I have seen the footage, Vincent. I know what I saw. You objected to the restriction in choice being imposed on you — a restriction which you *know* emanated as a direction from this building — and were therefore venting your frustration at the Ministry, the system."

"That's rubbish!"

"Is it? Is it?" Will points to him. "You say it's rubbish, yet here you sit in a red tie — a new bright red tie — perfectly happy to be seen doing so, to make a statement, to raise two fingers to authority."

"Is it illegal not to wear a blue tie?"

"Are you making a statement, Vincent? Is that what the tie is all about? Are you telling everyone that you're different or better — because that's what some of your colleagues think." Will glances to Verna for a second. "And not just Fran. Do you believe you should be living your life to a different set of standards?"

"Look, this is all nonsense." Vincent is unable to keep frustration from his voice. "What has all this got to do with the book?"

"Where did you get it?" Nowhere more than in room 1.49 is the answer to this question of interest. "Because you didn't get it from the outfitter's... So where,

Vincent? Where is there in the city currently selling bright red silk ties?"

Knowing the question could easily have been qualified with 'because they shouldn't be', Vincent shakes his head but says nothing.

"Or was it a gift from one of your lady-friends — perhaps for services rendered."

Slowly Vincent gets to his feet.

"Please sit down, Vincent." Will smiles. "The theatrical doesn't become you. And it is also — inappropriate."

Both standing, the two men stare at each other across the table for a few moments. Vincent, remembering Verna, looks her way hoping for a clue, some kind of interjection, but she remains motionless. He sits back down.

"Thank you." Will also resumes his seat. "And now you have answered my questions, I will answer yours: what has all this got to do with the book..."

Will glances to the corner of the room. Aware he is about to break protocol, were it in his eye-line he would have looked up to the camera for a fraction of a second if only to signify to Marcus that he knew what he was doing. In any event, he feels he has justification for his next question. "Verna, given you are his manager, how would you describe the job Vincent has done?"

Thrown by her sudden off-script inclusion, it takes a moment before Verna leans slightly forward. Vincent twists in his chair in order to be able to see her. In room 1.49 Marcus watches on.

"Me?" She considers. "Thorough, calculated, precise — just as Vincent's work always is."

"So nothing rushed about it? Or careless?"

"Definitely not. There are others who can waiver from time to time, but not Vincent."

She offers a slight smile which Vincent acknowledges by inclining his head; then he turns back to face Will, feeling vindicated.

"How does that make you feel, Vincent?"

"Satisfied, obviously. Proud, I suppose. I always try and do the best job I can; it's nice to know that it's recognised."

"Always? Since the very beginning of your time as a controller?"

"I'd like to think so."

"And would you say that your philosophy — outside of work I mean — has also been a constant?"

Vincent rests both his hands on the table. They are within touching distance of Frank's story, the book that is somehow responsible for this entire episode. For a moment he wishes he could pick it up and throw it away, as if doing so might negate the last week of his life. And then he remembers Marina. Not all of the last week then.

Will takes Vincent's silence for something it is not. "Well? Think about what you believe in, Vincent; is it the same now as when — say — you were working in non-fiction?"

"What's that got to do with it?"

"Do you remember a book you worked on, the one that offered a précis of recent European history: France, Germany and the like?"

"Yes, of course."

"And were you happy with what you produced? Did the tone of the book meet your objectives?"

The chair in room 1.49 creaks a little as Marcus shifts his position. In a nearby carpark, the slamming of a car door echoes toward the square.

"It was an accurate representation of what happened, totally aligned to the accepted history — if that's what you mean."

"I'm afraid it isn't. Oh the facts are right enough, but the whole book is riddled with bias. Was that deliberate?"

"Bias?"

"Towards those who would rise up: the freedom fighters in Spain during the Civil War, those of a more democratic bent in Nazi Germany, the various revolutions in some eastern European countries. You could easily have been more antiseptic in your approach, yet you were not. Was that deliberate, your bias? Did that represent the first stirrings of what you truly believe?"

Suddenly tired, Vincent's laugh is no more than half-hearted.

"You may well try to brush off your indiscretions, but some of us regard that volume as evidence — as valid as the testimony of Fran, the shop assistant, Mrs Carsington. Even your red tie!"

"Evidence?"

"What was it Verna just said? 'Thorough, calculated, precise'. Even when you were in non-fiction, you approached history with something of a slanted view."

"You're crazy!"

For a second Will waits, as if a switch has been flicked, brought the simmering towards boiling. Then he gathers himself.

Marcus knows they are reaching the tipping point. Will has played his hand well enough, even if pushing a little too hard; suggesting one thing but never quite ruling out the other.

Outside, a woman runs towards the Ministry's main entrance.

"Not crazy enough to not have been watching you; observing you on-and-off ever since then. Wondering whether there was something more to this slightly aloof controller. Still waters and all that..." Having regathered himself, Will pushes on. "You have a great deal to be proud of, a lot to show for your efforts. Like what you have done with this." Will looks down at the book laying on the table between them. "Another something you alone have achieved, without interference or aid. Careful, considered, thoughtful. Not a word out of place, you might say. Is that fair?"

There is something in the question Vincent finds a little odd. He wonders how words can be 'out of place', because if so, doesn't that suggest they may have a better or more appropriate place to be? Or that they can be inappropriately placed — which is, of course, an entirely different proposition altogether.

"Not how I would choose to phrase it, but as a generalisation I suppose it serves a purpose. Isn't that what we're paid to do anyway, put words in the right order?"

"And if there isn't a word out of place," Will continues with his theme, ignoring Vincent's comment, "then wouldn't it also be fair to say — given Verna's glowing reference on the quality of your work — that if we *were* to uncover a word that didn't quite seem at home then we might reasonably assume it was where it found itself with due cause, placed there with a specific purpose in mind?"

Vincent finds himself struggling with the vague personification of words upon which Will seems so insistent. Yes, they can be slippery and somehow unreliable at times — inconsistent even — but they are not emotional beings with Free Will, nor cattle or sheep a controller has to herd from one place to another.

Two doors down, Marcus shifts position in his chair. On the ground floor, satisfied by her credentials and excuse, Security allows a young woman access to the lifts.

"I'm not sure I follow you."

Will offers a hollow smile. "Humour me."

For Vincent, another strangely inappropriate turn of phrase.

"What do you think of the word 'justify', for example?" Will, having motioned to the book again, glances up, offers Vincent a quizzical look, attempting to suggest ignorance.

"I don't 'think' anything about it." Vincent is unable to mask his confusion. "It's just a word like any other. A tool, if you like, to enable a story to be told."

"Or something to be communicated?"

"Yes, of course."

When Will picks up the book, Vincent notices a series of small tags sticking out from between some of the pages. Obviously this is not his edit of the book, but presumably the version on which he worked, his source material.

"Take this." Settling on a tag, Will uses it to open the book and read. "*You've articulated what most people are thinking; justified the Government's actions.* Do you recognise that sentence Vincent?"

Now Vincent understands where this is going. Simultaneously Marcus sits up straighter in his chair. Elsewhere lift doors close.

"Most of the book becomes a blur, inevitably so, but some passages you remember; the difficult ones."

"Like this one?"

"The kitchen scene with Frank and his wife. Yes, I remember it."

"And do you remember the changes you made from the original?"

"Vaguely." Vincent tries to make his uncertainty sound authentic, suddenly unsure where boundaries between truth and falsehood lay.

Will reads from an inserted slip of paper. *"You've articulated what most people are thinking, tried to justify the Government's actions.* That's what is now written."

"Your point being?" As soon as they are out Vincent is aware that his words sound combative. Emitted, he can do nothing about them.

"Why did you change *justified the Government's actions* to *tried to justify the Government's actions*, Vincent?"

"You expect me to remember?"

"I expect you to have a reason."

"Perhaps because they read better, the sentence construction is improved?"

"Or because the message is clearer?" Will puts the book down.

"Frank's wife's message, you mean?"

"No, Vincent. Your message. Your message, Vincent. Your anti-Ministry message, using this fictional woman as your mouthpiece, to sow doubt, to ferment discontent. *Tried to justify*, Vincent; implying that the Ministry's actions couldn't be justified, not by Frank's wife, nor by Frank in his letter, nor by the Ministry itself."

Unable to stop himself, Vincent laughs.

"Laugh if you want to, but your revisions are full of these subtle little twists, explicit things most readers wouldn't notice but which collectively might work on them in the background." Will is speaking more quickly, with greater urgency.

Two doors away Marcus is standing, suddenly wondering if he has miscalculated — not about Vincent, but about Will — and whether Will has miscalculated too. There is something in his tone which suggests this is not merely play-acting, nor the charade with which they'd planned to test Vincent. This is full-on Simpsonesque accusation based on an unswerving belief in the Ministry's dogma. And Will is doing so assuming he has Marcus's backing, his support; that he is only doing what Marcus — a Ministry man these last nine years — would do.

Marcus has always assumed that they were on the same side, comrades-in-arms fighting their small war against the state, against people like Simpson; a war he used to wage with words put into the mouths of fictional characters. And a war he continues to wage secretly, from within the precincts of the Ministry itself, chipping away, always hoping to find those — like Vincent — who might just be able to aid the cause. Now showing his true colours, Will is not just attacking Vincent; whether he realises it or not, Will is attacking him. And Verna. And Marina.

"That's ridiculous!" Vincent turns as he protests, aiming to include Verna in the debate once again, seeking to find an ally. She knows how the process works, how diligent he is; surely she will stand up for him. "It's just a minor amendment to make the text flow a little more smoothly."

"And make the seditious message it conveys a little more potent!"

Will stands as he says this, edges forward. It is a movement which — threatening as it is — prevents Vincent from replying, from any further denial. And from confessing too. Prevents him from trying to explain that his editing of the text was driven by the revelations contained in a red tie, the kiss of a woman, and the promise they carried.

Just as he is about to draw his eyes away from the screen in front of him, Marcus hears running in the corridor outside; from the monitor he hears the door to room 1.51 open, sees both Vincent and Will turn towards it.

He is in the corridor when he hears the single shot.

＊

What is a father supposed to think under such circumstances? How many scenarios played through Marcus's mind in those few seconds spent in the wilderness between rooms 1.49 and 1.51 — and how many of those scenarios imagined tragedy involving Marina?

He is two paces inside the door when he stops. Immediately in front of him a body lies prone on the floor, its limbs askew as if it were a marionette whose strings had been cut.

Will.

On the other side of the table, Marina is in Vincent's arms; the shape of her suggesting she might have been about to collapse herself when her fall was arrested. Her head is buried in his chest, his head tight to her neck, her shoulders. Neither of them register Marcus's presence just yet.

His first instinct is to visually scan Marina for signs of injury — or a gun. Even though he heard only one shot, he half expects to see red blooming on her blouse, the colour of her blood somehow mingled with the red of Vincent's tie. Or perhaps find a trail leaking from beneath her sleeve, dripping down to an embryonic pool on the floor. But there is none. And her hand — her right hand at least — hangs loose, empty. Marina is right-handed; had she fired the shot, that is the hand she would have used. Assuming it is impossible for Vincent to have had access to a gun, Marcus assumes she has dropped the weapon, scans the floor, the area around the outline of Will's body, beneath the table. Marina ran in, saw what was happening, shot Will, collapsed. What other explanation could there be?

And then he remembers Verna.

Slowly Marcus turns to look into the corner of the room, the corner tucked away behind the door, beyond the camera's reach, and where there is sufficient space for a single chair — and for a single person to sit in it. Except Verna is no longer sitting. Her own right hand is extended, her fingers cradling the small revolver she has so recently retrieved from her bag; retrieved, raised, and fired. Marcus looks down at Will again and sees the bullet-hole in his back. He holds out his hand toward Verna, an action which shakes her from her reverie.

"I didn't know what he was going to do," she says as she releases the weapon into his hand. "He seemed suddenly crazed, angry like I'd never known him..." She looks Marcus full in the face for the first time. "You saw?"

"I saw."

"Then when Marina burst in..." It is another fragmented sentence. "I knew he was armed. I think he was armed... You can check his jacket. He's changed Marcus; I think he saw himself as executioner as well as judge..."

"You sensed what he was going to do?"

Verna nods. Marcus places her revolver into his jacket pocket then bends over Will's prostrate figure. There is a fraction of a pause before he checks his clothing, then another before he withdraws a pistol. He examines it briefly, slips it into another pocket.

"You may be right, Verna," Marcus says. "The safety was off."

"He would have shot Vincent?"

Marina's voice drags her father away from where he remains crouched over the fallen man. As he rises, she releases herself from her lover and moves to embrace him.

"I'm sorry," she says.

"For what?" Marcus strokes her hair, nods to Vincent as if that is sufficient expression of thanks.

"I feel like this is all my fault." She sobs. "If I hadn't..."

"Rubbish." Knowing he needs to gain control of the situation, Marcus is instantly business-like. "None of this is your fault. I was beginning to suspect that Will wasn't really on our side, even though he played the game so well. A Ministry man through and through. Always Simpson's man. If it hadn't been Vincent, it would have been someone else. And after Vincent, then probably me, Verna, you…" Still holding on to Marina, Marcus turns a little. "Thank you, Verna; I think you've saved us all. And Vincent, I fear I am the one who should be apologising; you should never have been put in this situation — and that is my doing."

Vincent steps forward, takes Marina's hand and eases her back into his arms.

"You assume it's a situation I don't want to be in. And I didn't, not at all. Not until I met Marina, was given the challenge, forced to make a choice." He glances down to where the book still rests on the table. "Maybe I was always going to open my eyes one day, to decide to fight just a little bit. You were the catalysts. All of you."

"Then you're on our side?" Marcus's hand inadvertently moves to the top of a pocket.

Vincent smiles.

"Of course; how can I not be? I had a good teacher."

❋

As he reaches the end of his presentation he is certain what will come next. The experience of the last six years has demonstrated as much, his utterance of "any questions?" instantly followed by a copse of student hands all wanting to hear about that afternoon. On more than one occasion he has tried to stall, to filibuster, but in the recent past has come to the conclusion that it is better to get it out of the way, to satisfy curiosity — the lust for drama — and then move on.

Today it is a young bespectacled woman in the second row. She is young enough to be his daughter.

"You were there the afternoon Will T. was shot?"

"I was, yes."

"What happened?" Crude, but to the point.

He looks around the auditorium; nearly thirty pairs of eyes fixed on him.

"Knowing I was coming here, I suspect you've all read the official accounts of that day." He smiles, encourages a gentle laugh.

"But the real story?" A voice from the back of the auditorium he cannot immediately locate.

"The real story is very little different, of course. It was a standard controller review of an edited novel, second edition. Will T. was leading the interview. As things went on he became more and more agitated, and although it wasn't immediately obvious as to why, it soon transpired that he was frustrated that the book should be so 'conventional' and fail to take the opportunity to reflect any alternative perspective other than the official one."

"He was a revolutionary?" The young woman again.

"You would never have known it. Perhaps this had been coming; that book the straw which broke the camel's back." A pause. "He became incensed. I think he felt that there was an opportunity to make a statement, take a stand; that the controller concerned had failed to do so and therefore let him — and everyone else — down.

Whether he arrived at that meeting with premeditation, who can say. He was reaching for his gun when the third person in the room (luckily a third person is always present for safety reasons) stopped him."

"Permanently." Another voice from the back, this time giving rise to more general laughter.

"Indeed. There was an inquiry of course. Both the controller and the person who actually pulled a trigger were exonerated. There were no other witnesses. For a while it was news-worthy. Now, less so. And the process for validation has changed somewhat since then."

He waits. Sometimes they move on; most often they do not.

"Were you scared? You might have been shot."

Vincent knows it doesn't matter who in the auditorium has asked the question.

"I didn't have time to be scared. It was all over in an instant. The following week or two was not easy, but after that…"

He glances down to his watch. They have ten more minutes then he will be free to leave. He will make his way to the carpark, get in the jeep, drive twenty minutes out of the city and home. "How did it go?" Marina will ask. Most likely she will be cradling one of their children. "The same as ever," he will say.

Vincent scans the rows of young people and thinks that in this year's cohort there are fewer young men wearing ties — and that those who are seem happy to embrace flashes of colour. He has seen a number of tattoos peeking out from beneath shirt sleeves. On the women, skirts are perhaps a little shorter, jewellery a little more in evidence.

Back at the house a now fully-retired and reclusive Marcus will ask him "how did it go?" too — but his will be a question from an entirely different register. He will be interested in the struggle, for evidence that they are making progress; and Vincent will mention the jewellery, the tattoos, the ties.

As Vincent points to a young man half-way back to ask the next question, he remembers something his father-in-law said to him on the eve of his and Marina's wedding: "A long slow fuse has been lit. Our job is to keep it alight, to keep the flame fanned. We may not witness the explosion, but some day there must be one."

Milton Keynes UK
Ingram Content Group UK Ltd.
UKHW012320110424
440929UK00001B/25